Frank Cottrell-Boyce

RUNAWAY ROBOT

WHEN THEY TOLD HIM
TO MAKE NEW FRIENDS,
THEY DIDN'T MEAN
FROM SCRATCH . . .

Illustrated by Steven Lenton

MACMILLAN CHILDREN'S BOOKS

First published 2019 by Macmillan Children's Books
an imprint of Pan Macmillan
20 New Wharf Road, London N1 9RR
Associated companies throughout the world
www.panmacmillan.com

ISBN 978-1-5098-5177-5 (HB)
ISBN 978-1-5098-9676-9 (TPB)

1 3 5 7 9 8 6 4 2

A CIP catalogue record for this book is available from the British Library.

Printed and bound by CPI Group (UK) Ltd, Croydon CR0 4YY

To Denny
A book about a better world for my (much) better half.

And to all the bionic heroes who are helping to build that future. May all your departures be thrilling and your arrivals glorious.

PROLOGUE

I'm part human/part machine.
I'm a bit bionic.
I'm like Wolverine.
You could call me Alfie Wolverine.

That's not true, by the way. Not going to lie: I'm not even one bit like Wolverine. 'I'm like Wolverine' is one of the things they teach you to say at Limb Lab during New Limb, New Life lessons. They worry people will laugh at you or start hating on you for being part mechanical, so they teach you a load of jokes and put-downs.

And, in case the jokes don't work, they teach you karate.

They even teach you what to think.

For instance, don't think too much about how your accident happened. Accidents happen. End of. Start talking about it, and you'll start thinking about it. Start thinking about it, and you'll soon be thinking bad thoughts such as, *Was it my fault? Why didn't I*

1

just . . . ? etc. Rule number one: don't talk about it. Talk about something else.

That's the advice.

So I'm not going to talk to you about me.

I'm going to talk to you about Eric.

Eric is missing.

There is no sign of him. Weird, because normally wherever Eric goes he leaves plenty of signs. For instance: broken doors, crushed wheelie bins, and, one time, a car stuck up a tree. (Controversial!)

Today, there is nothing. No clue. It's like he's evaporated. It's not like he would be easy to miss . . .

Eric is six foot six.

He likes to sing.

He's super polite.

He does as he's told.

He's made of metal.

When he's cheerful, his eyes light up. Literally.

When he's worried, he spits fire. Literally.

Eric tends to take thing literally.

He can prepare light snacks.

Get rid of unwanted guests.

He can be conveniently stored in a shed.

He is magnetic when anxious.

Everyone knows him.

No one has seen him.

The thing is, I really want to find him for you.

Eric always says if you lose something try to retrace your steps.

So I'm retracing my steps.

These are my steps . . .

STEP 1: I GATECRASHED A PARTY

If you're going to swerve school, swerve it with style. Find somewhere to swerve *to*. Somewhere actually better than school. There are certain people who swerve New Limb, New Life lessons (naming no names – Shatila Mars) and spend their day hiding in the little wooden house in the children's playground in Skyways Park, or sitting in the bus shelter at Concorde Circus until their bums go numb, and their phones die of boredom.

No! Don't do this!

Go somewhere warm and exciting with excellent facilities and free entertainment.

When I swerve school, I go to the airport.

You're probably disappointed that I swerve school at all. But, seriously – stay with me.

There was a day when I couldn't face seeing anyone. I didn't have a plan. I got almost to the school gates, and then I swerved. Literally.

I mooched back up to the Circus, which is not a proper circus, by the way. It's the name of a traffic island with a tree in the middle. There were no jugglers or fire-eaters to be seen, just the 10A bus waiting at the stop. Oh, and Shatila and her mates lounging under the tree. The minute they saw me, they scrambled to their feet like predators in a wildlife documentary.

I acted like I hadn't seen them and stepped on to the bus. The 10A is a driverless bus, so no one was going to ask me why I wasn't in school. I sat back to enjoy the ride.

Five stops later, we were outside the airport. Even though I've lived here all my life – even though the planes fly so low over our house we can see the big flaps on their wings moving – I'd never been to the actual airport until that day.

Shatila can tell the time of day just by looking up at passing planes. She'll be like, 'That's the ten forty-five departure for Amsterdam', or whatever.

My brain said, 'One does not simply walk into an airport. One needs tickets and passports and stuff.' But another voice in a different part of my head was going, 'Let's see what happens.'

I listened to that one.

I walked through the door, and I was in a magic kingdom.

On the bus, we'd passed shops and houses and people taking their dogs for a walk or pushing pushchairs. On this side of the airport doors, it was people in suits pulling little suitcases on wheels, families dressed for sunny days, people in uniform and people getting ready to fly. There was a departure board with the names of cities I'd only ever seen on telly: Paris, Rome, Prague. There were places I'd never even heard of. Places that sounded made up: Faroe, Knock, Riga. All the ordinary things – home, school, all that – they all felt far away and not really real. All these new places felt like they were just one step away.

Obviously if you're in departures you need to look as though you're going somewhere. Especially if you're a Year Seven with no grown-up. Even if you're going nowhere, Nowhere is a big place. It's best to narrow things down. Instead of going Nowhere, pick a particular destination and decide that is the place you're not going to.

That first time I decided not to go to Disney World, Florida, I got into the queue at Area C, Desk 23 for Miami. Then I just let myself chill. Everyone else was complaining about queuing, but I was loving it – just standing there, looking at the adverts and the people coming and going, and imagining myself flying off to Miami on a school day, instead of going to my ICT lesson.

I tried to figure out how the airport worked.

Maybe it's because I'm part machine myself, but I've noticed I've started to think about things as though they're machines. For instance, you could look at an airport as a kind of vacuum cleaner. It sucks people out of the city – off buses and out of cars – into metal tubes, then spits them into the sky. That's departures.

The airport has two settings: departures and arrivals.

Departures is all stress. Everyone's hurrying to get into the right tube before it flies off.

Arrivals, though, is all just chill. It sucks people out of the sky and sends them home.

Departures is full of people stressing and crying.

Arrivals is full of people being happy and crying.

Arrivals is a party.

And I gatecrashed the party that day, and the next day, and whenever I felt like it from then on.

People in arrivals aren't queuing to check in or for the baggage drop. They are mostly standing around, behind a barrier, staring at big automatic doors marked 'Arrivals'. Soon after a plane lands, people start piling through those doors, pulling their luggage after them. If the people waiting recognize the people arriving, they duck under the barrier, rush forward and hug them. A lot of people hold up signs for their arrivals to see. Mostly they're taxi drivers with just names on their cards, like 'Mr Soyinka'. Or people in suits holding 'Welcome to Delegates of the International Labradoodle Convention' placards. Some people make special colourful signs with messages like 'Welcome Back, Mum'. Once there was a man with a sign that said 'The Love of My Life', but I don't think the love was that mutual because he was there three days running and went home alone. Another time, a load of people turned up dressed as Imperial Stormtroopers with a banner that read 'Welcome to the Dark Side'.

There's a flower shop in arrivals called Up, Up and Bouquet, and a cafe called Many Happy Returns. Sometimes people have just settled down to eat there when their friends or family come through the doors. Nine times out of ten, they will jump up, have a hug and forget to go back to their food. When that happens, you can walk past the table and quietly minesweep handfuls of chips, or swipe one of those massive cups of Coke. Sadly no one ever seems to leave crisps. Not even Pringles.

The good things in life are just too portable.

The woman who runs the cafe wears a big badge that reads 'Feel Free to Ask About Our Meal Deal'. It's a lie. Everything about her says, Do Not Ask Me Anything – I've Got Paninis to Heat.

If you're going to gatecrash a party, you have to know how to blend in. Otherwise people start asking you things like, 'Why aren't you in school?' So I decided to make a sign of my own. Even though, of course, I wouldn't actually be waiting for anyone, a sign that says, 'Not Actually Waiting for Anyone' would attract the wrong kind of attention.

So that night I rooted around in the shed, found a big cardboard box – I think it had had a duvet in it once – ripped one panel off, wrote 'Welcome Home' on it with glitter pens, then spent ages trying to think of a name to put there. If you put an ordinary name like Kate, then you might end up with hundreds of Kates coming at you. So I didn't write 'Kate'. I wrote 'Kate' with a twist: *'Katja'*. It just popped into my head. That, I thought, is convincing. Unusual but convincing. I had no idea where it came from.

The next day, I was dangling it over the barricade when Feel Free strolled by me. Her body kept striding forward – *busy, busy* – but her head swivelled on her neck. She had noticed me. A few minutes later, she came back the other way, so I noticed her. What I also noticed was the name on her badge: Katja. So the name Katja had not popped into my head from nowhere at all. It was her name. It had got into my head without my realizing it. And now she was standing right in front of me looking down.

'My name's Katja,' she said. 'Are you waiting for me?'

'No. A different Katja. Auntie Katja.'

'Really? And is she coming today?'

'Yeah. This flight. From Knock. Look, it's just landed. Won't be long now . . .'

'She's a busy woman, your auntie, isn't she? You were here yesterday. And the day before . . . and last week. You seem to have been hanging around the airport waiting for her for days. Why aren't you in school?'

She grabbed my hand. I tried to slip her grip, but she was definitely never going to let go.

So I did the only thing I could.

I let go of my hand.

I flipped the catch on my wrist that holds my hand in place and ran off, leaving my right hand behind in her left hand. I looked back just long enough to see her staring down in horror at what she was holding.

She looked up at me in shock.

She probably didn't know my right hand was detachable. She probably thought my arm was spurting blood. She dropped my hand as though it was blazing hot. It clattered to the floor.

'Your hand!' she shouted. 'Come back! You've dropped your hand.'

STEP 2: OK, I LOST MY HAND

I'm not Wolverine.

But I am part machine and slightly bionic.

My hand is detachable. State of the art. It came from a special factory in Hungary by 3D printer. It was given to me by Dr Shilling at the Limb Lab.

The Limb Lab is in a kind of glass bubble in the courtyard of a sprawling old house near Hangar Wood. The entrance hall has got swords and shields and coats of arms along its walls. It even has a propeller from an old-fashioned aeroplane, because the man who used to live here made his money building aeroplanes. There's

a fireplace the size of a tennis court with a Latin motto – *Felix Culpa* – carved over the mantelpiece.

I used to think Felix Culpa was the name of the man who lived there, but Dr Shilling explained that it was Latin for 'Happy Accident', which is annoying, because nearly everyone at the Limb Lab had had an accident, and none of them were happy.

Felix Culpa was the motto of her family, the Shillings. The man who built the aeroplanes was Dr Shilling's grandfather. After a while, he switched from building planes to making artificial body parts. Back then, the old house was in the middle of a country estate with trees and lakes and cows and deer. The kind of place where ladies with big hats go horse riding, and men with big beards go on shooting parties.

That's all gone now. They built the airport and the Skyways housing estate on it. But the old house is still there. That's called Shilling House Bionics. It's where they design all kinds of state-of-the-art bodily appendages: not just arms and legs, but hands, fingers, toes . . .

'And I'm proud to say there's still one Shilling working here – namely me,' says Dr Shilling. 'I am the last of the Shillings.'

The Limb Lab is the bit inside the glass bubble. That's where kids like me go to learn to use their new legs, hands, fingers or whatever they've had replaced. From the outside, it looks like a goldfish bowl. From the inside, it also looks like a goldfish bowl – only this time, you are the goldfish. You can also have normal lessons in there until you're ready to go back to school. There's even a Limb Lab uniform: short-sleeved shirt with a pocket for pens and rulers like an actual scientist.

'Because,' says Dr Shilling, 'here at the Limb Lab, we don't have patients. We don't have customers. We have co-researchers. This is a journey, and we travel together.'

The day my hand arrived, Dr Shilling let me watch it downloading. The whole hand just sort of happened, bit by bit, on a table in the Limb Lab, like it was beaming down from space. It took hours to materialize. Dr Shilling bent over it the whole time like a big Anglepoise lamp. She thinks Limb Lab's replacement body parts are way, way better than ordinary human ones. She calls the ordinary ones 'flesh jobs'. She calls the new ones by their model names. My right hand is an Osprey Grip MM.

'Look at that Osprey Grip MM,' she'd said with a sigh when it was finished. 'Isn't she the best?'

To be honest, it looked like something that had dropped off a shop dummy if the shop dummy was made of Lego. When I had to touch it, its coldness completely triggered me. It nearly made me remember the last time I saw my hand-hand, which is when it was flying through the air over my head before it splat-landed next to me. I was lying on my back on the ground. At the time, I couldn't figure out how I'd ended up on the ground. Or how my hand had ended up in the air. Didn't we usually stick together?

That's what I asked Dr Shilling about when she said, 'Any questions?'

'Did it land somewhere? Did someone pick it up? Did they try to put it back on?'

'I mean questions about your new hand,' said Dr Shilling. 'Not your old one. Your old one is in the past. Most of your memory is stored in your brain, but some of it is stored in your muscles – that's why you can do some things without thinking about them. You lost your hand. And some of your memory went with it. You're getting a new hand. You'll make new memories after a while. Maybe your old memories will be recovered. Maybe they won't. Until then, enjoy your brand-new hand.'

She tried to show me how to attach the hand.

It didn't fit.

Dr Shilling couldn't understand it. 'It's a perfect copy,' she said. 'We did it with lasers.'

Like I said, because I'm part machine, I'm usually good at thinking about machines and how they work.

'This is a perfect copy,' I said, 'of my left hand.'

'An absolutely perfect copy,' said Dr Shilling, 'of . . . Oh. Ha! I see what you're saying! Very good, Alfie! We've given you two left hands. We forgot to reverse the template.'

When the right version came a few days later, it fitted OK, but I couldn't really work it.

As long I don't look at my empty wrist, I can still feel my old hand there. I mean, I know it's gone. I saw it flying off into the air. Fairly unforgettable sight. If I lift my arm and look at my wrist, I can see that it's totally hand-free. But as long as I don't look, I can still feel it. I mean, *really* feel it. I can wriggle fingers that aren't there, clench an impossible fist, point, feel the cold, feel the heat . . .

'What you're feeling,' explained Dr Shilling, 'is not your hand. It's the ghost of your hand. That is completely normal. Ask the others.'

Oh. The others.

I'd better tell you about the others. 'The others' refers to everyone who goes to the Limb Lab. Obviously they've all got state-of-the-art body parts. Some have got new hands, some new legs, some both. There's actually a kind of league table. Your ranking depends on two things:

17

How cool is/are your new body part/s?
How good is the story of how you lost your original body part/s?

Bottom of the league is probably Tyler.

Tyler lost a few fingers when he went over to take a closer look at a lit firework that hadn't gone off. He picked it up and gave it a shake. It went off then, and it took three of his fingers with it. Why is he even *in* the Limb Lab? He should be in a 'Don't Mess With Fireworks' class. He sometimes refers to himself as 'The Tyler'. He walks with his head down, like he's looking for something he recently dropped.

In the middle of the league table, we have D'Arcy.

D'Arcy lost the lower half of both her legs, and now she has blades instead. There are quite a few people with blades in and out of the lab, but she lost her legs in a famous incident when a funfair zip wire came unzipped. So her story was in all the papers. Twice. Once when it happened, and then again when she was the 'brave little girl who everyone thought would never walk again'. Having your story in the papers is impressive.

Top of the table, no question, is Shatila Mars (otherwise known as Shatter).

You can't even tell that Shatter has a new body part, unless you know where to look. It's a new foot, by the way. A more than averagely impressive foot. But what makes Shatter top of the table is that she lost her foot when it was blown off as she stepped on a landmine back home in Bosnia, where she's from.

She's a victim of war, which is more impressive than being in the papers, and massively more impressive than being stupid around fireworks.

Shatter's foot arrived by 3D printer too. It was made of resin in exactly the same colour as Shatter's deep-brown skin. Except for the toes which were shiny metal.

'Shatila is going to help us test and refine it,' said Dr Shilling, 'and when we've got it just right we can send hundreds of them by printer to other disabled children in her home country, and she can go and be an inspiration to them all.'

Shatter not only says whatever she feels like saying; she says it with as many full stops as she wants, and she puts them wherever she wants. It's as though life has given her an excessive amount of punctuation, and she's trying to get rid of it.

For instance, the first time she met me, she said, 'Who are. You? And what are. You for?'

What am I for? What is anyone for? I still wake up thinking about that.

Apparently she talks like that because that's the way she was taught to speak English. I once asked her who taught her to speak like that, with all the unexpected full. Stops.

'No one. I. Taught. Myself,' she said.

'But how?'

'I asked Alexa. Questions in. English and. Copied the. Answers.'

So she basically learned English from a robot, and now she talks like one.

After Dr Shilling said that about her being *an inspiration*, Shatter said, 'My foot is. Itchy.'

'Gross,' said D'Arcy.

'Are you. Calling my. Foot gross?'

'The itching is probably caused by sweat,' said Dr Shilling.

'Double gross,' said D'Arcy.

'Are you. Calling my. Foot double. Gross?' Shatter threw a karate kick, her brand-new foot stopping just a quivering breath away from D'Arcy's nose. 'This. Foot?' said Shatter.

'Yes,' said D'Arcy. 'But close up it's not gross at all. Close up it's a lovely foot.'

'Lovely. Foot,' said Shatter. 'Don't for. Get it.'

Settling discussions by means of fear is her great talent.

Her other talent is knowing where an aeroplane is coming from or going to, just by looking up when it flies past. Honestly, you can be sitting in the Tranquillity

Garden and a plane will go by and she will look up and say, 'KLM mid-morning flight. From Zurich.' Amazing.

'Of course,' said D'Arcy one time, 'we don't know if she's always right or not. About those planes.'

'If you really wanted to be sure,' said Tyler, 'you could ask her to prove it.'

We all agreed that we would prefer to give her the benefit of the doubt.

A few days after my hand arrived, Dr Shilling brought a visitor into the classroom.

'This is Mo,' she said. 'He's a student of engineering at university. He wanted to meet you. And I think you wanted to show the children something, Mo – is that right?'

'A card trick.' Mo smiled. 'Just for you. Here's my pack of cards.'

He pulled open the pack and shuffled the cards. I mean *really* shuffled them, like a proper magician, fanning them out, letting them cascade from hand to hand, spreading them out, flicking them over. Then he looked up at us. We sat waiting for him to say 'pick a card', or whatever.

'Are you. Going to do this. Magic trick. Ever?' asked Shatter.

'Done already,' said Mo, smiling broadly.

Everyone looked around, wondering if a rabbit had

appeared in the room or something.

'I shuffled those cards,' said Mo, 'with *this*.' He rolled up his sleeve.

We all saw that the bottom part of his arm was made of some kind of transparent plastic. You could see that it didn't have muscles and bones, but wires.

Even Shatter was mildly impressed.

'I am mildly. Impressed,' she said.

Everyone who had two hands clapped. Everyone who had a foot to stamp stamped. It looked like real magic.

'This is not magic,' said Dr Shilling. 'You will all learn to do this. Mo was a student here at the Limb Lab. Just like you. He lost his hand during the rebellion in Sierra Leone. His new hand has a blue-tooth connection chipped into his upper arm.'

'I'm moving this hand with my mind,' explained Mo. 'Just like I did with my old flesh job hand. Alfie, when you first lost your hand, could you feel a ghost hand where it used to be?'

'Yeah.'

'Can you still feel it sometimes?'

'All the time.'

'Can you still feel it when you have your new hand on?'

'Yes.'

'How does it feel?'

'Like a ghost trapped in a box.'

'That's how it was for me too,' said Mo.

'The truth is,' explained Dr Shilling, 'we all have a ghost hand. It's just that usually it's in the same place as our flesh hand. Your ghost hand wore your flesh hand like a glove. It was the ghost that made the flesh hand work. All you have to do is let your ghost hand make your new hand work. Just let yourself feel your ghost hand for a while. Then, when I tell you to, put your Osprey Grip back on.'

I did as she said.

Don't get me wrong, the Osprey Grip hand is amazing. You can get it to do all kinds of stuff. But you can't get it to feel anything. You can't use it to tell if a thing is wet or dry or hard or soft or hot or cold.

The moment I take it off, I can feel again. Even though my hand's not there, I can feel the breeze on its non-existent back, and the hard wood of the chair on its non-existent knuckles.

'Ready? OK. Keep your ghost hand in mind and now put your Osprey back on.'

Once again, I did as she said.

'Right. Now try to use your ghost hand to lift your Osprey hand. Don't use any of the muscle tricks that you've learned here at the Limb Lab – just try to imagine your ghost hand lifting it.'

I tried. Nothing happened. The ghost hand was in there, moving around, but it just wasn't strong enough to move the Osprey hand.

'Come on. Give it a go.'

'I'm . . . giving . . . it . . . a . . . go.'

The Osprey hand just hung down at my side, heavy as a really heavy hammer.

'Look at my. Foot,' said Shatter. She stuck her foot out. 'Twiddling my. Toes.'

I swear she really was twiddling her toes.

'She's twiddling her toes,' said Tyler, who seemed to have decided that it was his job to translate everything Shatter said.

Ten seconds later, Shatter was doing keepy-ups with the lab practice ball.

'Doing keepy. Ups,' she said.

'Shatter is doing keepy-ups,' explained Tyler.

Do you know what it was like? Remember in *Harry Potter and the Philosopher's Stone* when they're learning the levitation charm, trying to make a feather take off. And no one can do it. Then Hermione just goes, '*Wingardium Leviosa*,' and her feather takes off round the room? Well, it was just like that. Shatter was Hermione, and I was Ron.

I tried again. This time, something happened.

Like a spirit walking through a door, my ghost hand just passed through the side of the Osprey hand. Just straight through it. And then it just smoked off into the air. Just evaporated. For the first time since I lost my hand, I couldn't feel anything at the end of my arm. Just an empty space with a plastic thing strapped to it.

I may be good with machines generally, but there's one machine I haven't mastered yet. And that's the Osprey Grip.

'Don't worry, Alfie. Not everyone gets it first time.' Dr Shilling patted my shoulder. 'When you go home, get a big pile of Lego and start building with it. We often find that when people are playing Lego they get so absorbed in what they're building they forget to think about what the hand is doing. And that's when it starts to really work – when you're not thinking about it.'

There's a little table at home that usually has a plant pot and a lamp on it. When I got home, Mum cleared it, then emptied a tub of Lego out on to it.

'When you can build a little house out of Lego, we'll know you're on your way,' she said, smiling encouragingly.

I did try. Playing with Lego was supposed to make you forget about your hand. Instead it just made me think about my hand even more and forget about the Lego. It also made me think about what Shatter had said: '*What are you FOR?*'

Apparently I was not for building Lego.

What *was* I for, then? Everyone else in the Limb Lab was really getting into being slightly bionic. I thought about jacking in the lab and going back to my old school. But school was full of people like Thursday Wells, who would happily flush your head down the toilet if you were wearing the wrong deodorant. Imagine what they'd do if you had the wrong type of hand. The truth is, I was too bionic for school. Not bionic enough for the Limb Lab, though. I was a prisoner of the hand.

So when the woman from the Many Happy Returns cafe grabbed it in the airport arrivals hall I unfastened it and ran.

STEP 3: LOST PROPERTY

I ran off into departures. If you've got a ticket and a passport, you could run into departures and end up in Miami. Me, I ended up running slap bang into the chest of a security guard. Not quite into his chest, to be honest – more into his beard. It was very long and so thick and vast that he seemed more beard than person. A beard in uniform. A talking beard.

'No running in the airport,' the beard said.

'Sorry – I just . . .'

'Where are your parents?'

I could see the face behind the beard now.

'They're not here.'

'Are you an unaccompanied minor?'

I wasn't sure what that was, but it didn't sound good.

He tutted. 'You'd better come with me.'

I really didn't want to do that, so I lifted up my arm and said, 'I lost my hand!'

The security guard jumped back in a flurry of beard, his head swivelling as if he was looking for my hand, except he was looking at the ceiling. If there was a disembodied hand bleeding all over the floor, he really didn't want to see it.

'Sorry, sorry,' he said. 'I'll get a doctor.'

'No. No. It's a special hand. Made of plastic.'

'A toy hand?'

'No. My hand that I use. It goes here. Look . . .' I pushed back my sleeve so he could see where it was missing.

'You've got a false hand?'

'It's not false. It's a real hand, but plastic. Prosthetic. An Osprey Grip MM hand.'

He was so relieved that he started being actually helpful. 'Let me see if I can . . . I mean, I'll ask if anyone's seen . . . I mean . . . What does it look like?'

'A hand.'

'Yes. Of course it does.'

'But more Lego-ish than most hands.'

'Right. Follow me.'

And he led me through the forbidden door.

I mean he led me through the big doors marked 'Arrivals'. You can normally only walk through them from the other side – when you're arriving. I'd never seen anyone walk through them from this side.

There were rows of conveyor belts with suitcases toddling along them. Crowds of people stood around waiting to collect them, like grown-ups waiting for their kids at the school gates. We walked past the conveyor belts into a corridor that was so narrow it felt more like a tube. Beardy Security kept checking over his shoulder, making sure I was following him. We finally came to a metal door. He opened it with a code, and then we were in an area signed 'Lost Property'.

The first time I walked into the airport, I thought it was a magic kingdom. But Lost Property – well, Lost Property is an Aladdin's cave.

There's a desk, and behind the desk sat a woman in a crisp red uniform, with the biggest Afro you've ever seen. She had a badge on her lapel that said 'Happy to Help'. This must have been her actual name because it definitely wasn't a description of her mood. Her Afro looked like her own personal thundercloud. She kept looking at her tablet the way the wicked queen in Snow White kept looking in her mirror.

'He's lost a hand,' said the security guard.

'Lost hand,' muttered the thundercloud in a voice that implied people were constantly losing their hands, and she was bored of it. 'Left or right?'

I held up my right arm so she could see my hand was missing, but she didn't look up from her tablet.

'Right,' I said.

'Right,' she said to her computer.

'*Right*,' replied her tablet in a voice that sounded

a bit like the snowman in *Frozen*. *'Is the owner losing blood?'*

'Are you losing blood?' said Happy to Help. 'Do you need medical attention?'

'No. It's a detachable hand. It came off in someone else's hand. In arrivals. By the cafe.'

Now the woman looked up at me. 'Are you saying it's been stolen? Because if it's been stolen that's a police matter.'

'She wasn't stealing it. It was an accident. The lady didn't know the hand was detachable.'

'Hmmm,' said Happy to Help.

'*Size?*' said the computer.

'Size?' repeated Happy to Help.

'She was about average height,' I said.

'Size,' sneered Happy to Help, 'of the *hand*. This is Lost Property, not Scotland Yard.'

I held up my left hand for her to see and said, 'Same size as this one.'

She peered at my hand for a second and said, 'Child-sized. How many fingers?'

'Normal number. Five including a thumb.'

'Any distinguishing features – wedding rings or such?'

'I'm not married. I'm twelve.'

'Right.' She swiped the screen and waited. 'It seems we have had a number of hands HANDED in.'

I waited for her to tell me more, but she paused and stared at me, like her mind was buffering.

'Hands. Handed in? Hello? Joke.'

'Oh. Yes. Very funny.'

'We have a pair of hands in aisle eleven, which are tartan with little bobbles on the back. The fingers are like little Loch Ness Monsters and . . .'

'I think they're probably gloves.'

She peered at me. Then she peered at her tablet. 'You may well be right,' she said. 'Blue leather hand with pearl buttons at the wrist and . . . That's a glove too, isn't it?'

'Think so.'

'So much for image recognition.' She swiped the screen a few times, muttering. 'Glove . . . Another glove . . . That's a doll . . . That's not even a hand – that's hand *cream* . . . What is wrong with you!' she yelled at the screen.

'*Sorry, guys,*' said her tablet in a frightened voice. '*Searches seem to be fuzzier than usual today.*'

Happy to Help swiped the screen, but quickly, like a slap.

The tablet said, '*You are exhibiting signs of stress. Why not try taking a few deep breaths. Be mindful. Aisle fourteen. One hand.*'

'Come with me,' said Happy to Help.

Arrivals is a properly noisy place. People are

cheering and crying. Phones are going. There are announcements every couple of minutes. Lost Property, on the other hand, is seriously quiet. The only sound was of Happy to Help's heels on the tiles. *Tut tut tut*, they went, as though they were disgusted with the whole idea of walking.

I followed her down a corridor of shelves – long shelves, stretching miles into the distance and high over our heads. Shelves crowded with plastic boxes labelled with words like 'Umbrellas', 'Phones' and 'Teeth'. Sometimes, through a gap, I could see that there were other shelves. Shelves beyond shelves. Shelves stretching to the left and right – like lanes in an infinite bowling alley.

Everything here had been forgotten. Pushchairs, wheelchairs, luggage and laptops. Metre upon metre of lost dolls and teddy bears. Their brown eyes seemed to follow us as we passed, like they were saying, *Come and stay with us in the Land of Forgotten Toys. Forever.*

'Stick close to me,' said Happy to Help over her shoulder. 'The lights are activated by my presence. It can get very dark in the shelves when I'm not here. People have been known to get lost in Lost Property. I've got an app that takes me to the selected item. See?'

I chased after the pool of light that swirled out around her tutting feet.

There was a coffin on one of the shelves we passed.

I hoped that it was empty. Two aisles over, something that looked like the helmet from a suit of armour was lying on its side. She just breezed past it. I swear the head shifted on the shelf, watching us go by. OK, that could just have been the light moving.

Her phone said, '*Your selected item is on the left.*'

Happy to Help stopped and looked.

'*One hand,*' said the phone. '*Happy to have helped.*'

She motioned to me to pick up the hand and tutted quickly towards the exit.

There was a hand on the shelf all right, but it wasn't my hand. It was huge. Three times the size of a human hand. It had long pointy fingers made of jointed steel. When I tried to pick it up, it was so heavy I could hardly lift it, let alone carry it. Not with my one remaining hand, anyway. So I had to rest it on my shoulder like a soldier carrying a rifle and follow her back the way we came. I had to rush to catch up with her, or I would have been locked in there forever, lost as that long-lost coffin.

We passed the helmet thing again. It was looking at me. Again. Only this time it wasn't a trick of the light. Its eyes flickered blue. I tried to hurry past it. Happy to Help was way ahead now. The light followed her. I could see the cone of light ahead, but everything around me was in darkness—

Then out of that darkness something grabbed me.

I didn't want to look, but I had to.

A metal hand! But this one was on the end of a metal arm. And the metal arm was attached to the shoulder of a massive metal body. The massive metal body was lying flat on the shelf. At one end of the metal body was the helmet with the flickering blue eyes. Armadillo-style plated steel fingers curled round my flesh. The hand moved my hand up and down.

I was nearly rigid with fear. Then something flashed across my brain. 'Are you,' I said, 'shaking hands with me?'

I AM THE WORLD'S MOST POLITE ROBOT.

I'm used to that voice now. But the first time I heard it, it was a bit of a shock. It's a voice that could stop traffic. I wish you could hear it. A mixture of wind and steel – like bagpipes playing inside a washing machine. But with words.

'Is this your hand?' I asked, turning round so it could see the hand hanging over my shoulder.

I CAN ANSWER ALMOST ANY QUESTION.

'Is this your hand?'

SORRY. I AM UNABLE TO ANSWER THAT QUESTION.

The helmet turned towards me. Two eyes set in two huge, dark pits sparked blue as they saw me. The mouth was as wide as a letterbox and burned an electric-fire yellow when he spoke. Imagine looking

into the slot of a toaster, and you'll know what I mean. In fact, there was a slight smell of burning electricity about him.

I tried to stay calm. I could see that there was a catch inside the metal hand that more or less matched another catch inside his handless wrist.

'Hold your wrist up,' I said.

I AM YOUR OBEDIENT SERVANT.

'Great. I've never had a servant before. Do you know how this fastens?'

I AM THE WORLD'S MOST KNOWLEDGE-ABLE ROBOT.

'So DO you know how to put your hand back on, then?'

I AM SORRY. I AM UNABLE TO ANSWER THAT QUESTION. AND NOW . . . THE NATIONAL ANTHEM, 'GOD SAVE OUR GRACIOUS KING . . .'

Then this thing started to sing. Well, not *sing*, exactly, but I don't know what else to call the noise it was making. It wasn't like human singing. More like a tractor singing with a backing track of steam and hammers. Surely, I thought, when she heard all the noise, Happy to Help would come back and help me out of this situation . . .

Then – mid chorus – it stopped singing and leaned forward, as though thinking of something.

IT IS GOOD MANNERS TO STAND DURING THE NATIONAL ANTHEM.

'I AM standing. You're the one who's sitting down.'

The metal suit didn't speak or move. Maybe I'd been a bit rude. Can you be rude to a chunk of metal? I tried to make up for it by starting a different conversation.

'Are you in Lost Property because you've lost something? Or are you in Lost Property because you're lost? I mean, are you the lost thing or the loser?'

I HAVE GOT LOST.

Inside the suit, I could hear cogs clicking and wheels whirring. I thought it might be the sound of robot tears. I said, 'Shall we try to put your hand back on?' Thinking this might cheer it up.

But it was not the sound of robot tears. It was the sound of robot effort as he tried to stand up. Its eyes flashed blue. Its mouth burned bright orange. The helmet ducked into the aisle. Arms reached out. One leg steadied itself on the floor. Then . . .

I was waiting for the other leg to appear but there was no other leg.

'Whoa!' I said. 'Don't stand up. You've only got one leg.'

IT IS CUSTOMARY TO STAND DURING THE NATIONAL ANTHEM.

'Yeah, but you've only got one leg. You're going to

fall. On top of me. You're going to kill me . . .'

It tried to steady itself by planting a hand on the shelf. Its head rose up.

And up.

And up.

'My days,' I said. 'You're huge!'

GOD SAVE THE KING!

'And loud. You're really, really loud.'

The shelves shook. In their boxes, the lost teeth chattered. The mislaid coffin shuddered as if the body was going to climb out of it. Lost luggage trembled.

Suddenly it let go of the shelf and nodded its head. At least, it was a nod to start with, but then it became a topple. Eyes flashing, teeth blazing, mouth roaring . . .

LONG LIVE OUR NOBLE KING . . .

Its massive face was crashing towards me. Something flashed across my brain. Something familiar.

What was it?

Oh. Yes.

That was it.

Fear.

Absolute, extreme fear.

STEP 3 AGAIN (I missed a step): ABSOLUTE EXTREME FEAR

There's a gap in my memory here. I do remember the robot falling like a massive mallet towards me. The next thing I remember was being in a little room with someone in a medical uniform asking me to follow their finger with my eyes while Happy to Help watched anxiously from the doorway. The medical woman said that I was fine physically but in a state of shock. Then she asked me who I had come to the airport with. I wasn't going to admit that I was just hanging around the airport on my own, minesweeping food. But I couldn't think of anything else to say.

'Shock,' said the medical woman in an understanding way when I didn't reply. 'Were you going on holiday? Do you remember where?' She had started to speak very slowly. She seemed to believe that a state of shock might turn a person into a two-year-old. 'Can't you remember?'

I shook my head. It was true that, at that point, I was having a lot of trouble remembering things.

'Definitely,' she said. 'Shock.' She looked at her wristwatch. 'Odd. My watch is supposed to ping if anyone is reported missing. Oh well. We'll keep you here and give you a nice big cup of tea until you start to feel better. Meantime, no doubt someone is looking for you in the airport. I'm sure we'll get an update soon.'

Happy to Help brought over the robot's shovel-sized hand. She put it on my lap as though it was my missing hand and started to go on about how none of this was her fault.

'A robot fell on him,' she said.

'A *robot*?' said the medical person.

'Yeah. It's listed on the database as a suit of armour. And it looks like it's been there for *years*. I'm getting Health and Safety to move it right away.'

The medical woman kept looking at her watch. 'It's still not pinged,' she huffed. 'I'm going to send a notification, and if there's no reply we'll have to take you to the hospital. What's your name?'

I had been feeling a bit foggy, but as soon as she said the word 'hospital' my brain became very clear indeed. That sounded like trouble. So I just nodded at her.

'You don't know your name?'

'Can you give me a clue?' I asked.

The medical woman sucked her teeth. 'This is worse than I thought,' she said.

'Can I go to the toilet?'

'Of course. It's just across the corridor. Don't forget your hand!'

As soon as I was in the corridor, I ran, clutching the big metal hand under my arm. I dodged past the passengers and exited through the big automatic door that opened into arrivals.

When the doors opened, I had to take a step back. All those eyes staring at me – I really wasn't ready for that. Every single head behind the barrier scanned me, checking to see if I was the person they were waiting for.

For a second – with all those eyes on me – I felt like a celebrity. Then the eyes all decided I wasn't the person they were waiting for and looked away. Except for a few who carried on staring at the big armoured fist I was carrying.

It's not easy to carry a giant steel hand if you've only got one hand yourself.

I settled it deeper under my arm, and tried to stroll on, as if it was the most normal thing in the world.

STEP 4: DO. NOT. LET. GO.

You know when you forget your coat? Or leave your phone at your mate's house? And your mum says, 'Where's your coat?' And you say, 'Oh! Sorry – I forgot it.' And you promise to get it back the next day.

It's not the same if you leave your hand behind.

If you lose your flesh-job hand, people come running round to take you to hospital, send you cards, say nice things and – in the end – fix you up with a brand-new state-of-the-art replacement hand.

If you lose your brand-new state-of-the-art replacement hand, they're not going to be nice about it. Leave your state-of-the-art hand somewhere, and difficult questions will be asked.

And the answer to one of those questions will have to include, 'I swerved school and went to the airport.' Which is not a sentence you ever want to have to say to your mum.

There was no way I could leave the airport without my hand.

Luckily the Osprey Grip MM has its own little app

that synchs with your phone. It's called HandShake. It looks like a hand with its fingers spread out. The fingers disappear one by one as the hand's battery fades. It's also got a 'Where's My Hand?' button, which helps you locate your hand.

Turns out, my hand was still on five fingers' worth of battery. And it was still in the airport. And I probably would have found it if one of those electric luggage buggies hadn't come between me and the door. Its klaxon was beeping. It kept saying, '*Excuse me, please. Unstable load. Thank you.*'

I stepped out of its way and saw what the unstable load was.

It was the robot.

It lay across the back of the trolley. It wasn't dead because it had never been alive, but it really did look dead. Its joints chimed like church bells when the trolley stopped to wait for the airport doors to open. I followed the trolley down the ramp. It crossed the short stay car park, heading for the multi-storey.

When the trolley stopped by the service lift, the robot's head turned towards me. The lift doors opened. The trolley wheeled itself inside, still saying, '*Unstable load. Thank you.*'

As the lift doors began to close, the robot's eyes flickered. It was staring at my hand.

No, not at *my* hand. At its own huge metal hand.

44

Was it asking for its hand back?

The lift doors closed.

The robot vanished from sight.

I could have turned round then and walked away.

But I didn't.

I had to give him his hand back.

I charged up the stairs.

I chased the lift up to the roof.

If I hadn't done that, none of this would have happened.

The trolley had already trundled out of the lift by the time I got to the rooftop. It had parked itself in the middle of the wide, empty space. It was proper windy up there, and noisy – like someone was beating the air with a massive whisk. I didn't notice what was causing that at first. All I noticed was the robot. It wasn't lying on the trolley any more. It was standing up on one leg. On tip-toe, like an armoured ballet dancer.

'Hey!' I shouted, over the noise.

Then I saw the helicopter, hovering right over his head. That's where the noise was coming from. It was small and white with POLICE painted on its side in black letters.

The robot's toes drifted off the floor. He was floating up into the air, swinging like a pendulum, every swing taking him a little bit higher.

A long cable dangled from the helicopter's hatch, like a fishing line.

Then I realized. The robot was attached to the end of the cable.

'I brought your hand back!' I shouted over the noise.

THANK YOU.

It really was a polite robot. Even when it was dangling from a long metal cable, suspended from the belly of a helicopter, it remembered to say thank you. As it twisted in the air above me, it held its one hand out towards me.

'Oh right! Sorry! Nearly forgot!'

It wasn't easy, fixing the hand back on the dangling robot's wrist, especially as I only had one hand myself. The robot helped me by twisting its wrist on to the thread inside the hand. He held out his hand for me to shake.

I made a grab for it with my right hand, totally forgetting I didn't actually have a right hand. Just the ghost of a right hand. It passed through the air like light through a window.

Then something grabbed me by the wrist and hoisted me into the air. The robot. He lifted me level with his face and stared into my eyes.

'Hi,' I said, under his blazing blue gaze.

I was about to say, *'I think I'd like to get down now,'* when I realized I was no longer dangling three metres

above the roof of the multi-storey. The helicopter had moved over the edge. I was now suspended about thirty metres above the tarmac. The runways spread out beneath me. Planes were queuing up for take-off. Lego–sized people were hurrying around. I tried not to look.

'We're going to fall,' I said. 'We're going to plunge to our doom.'

The robot put his hand under my arm and hoisted me up to his chest.

MY NAME IS ERIC. HOW DO YOU DO? WHO ARE YOU?

'Hi, Eric,' I said. 'I'm Alfie. PLEASE. Do. Not. Let. Go . . .'

I AM YOUR OBEDIENT SERVANT.

We swung out high over the Skyways estate. Hey. Guess what. The whole estate – the roads and avenues – was shaped like one massive aeroplane spread out on the ground. That's what it looks like to people arriving at the airport – a gigantic aeroplane.

'Where are we going?' I wondered out loud.

I CAN ANSWER ANY QUESTION.

'So, where *are* we going?'

I'M SORRY, I CAN'T ANSWER THAT QUESTION.

STEP 5: SKYWAYS

Skyways is now the most advanced state-of-the-art housing estate in Europe. All the houses are super insulated, super solar-heated and super intelligent. When you open the front door, the house says '*Hello*' and switches on the heating and the kettle and the CCTV for you. When it's time for bed, the house dims the lights and switches off all screens.

And, of course, it's right next to the airport because it all started with the airport. Old Mr Shilling used to build aeroplanes in a hangar on his estate. Planes with names like *Excalibur* and *Guinevere* because he loved anything to do with knights and chivalry. Back then, they used to call pilots 'knights of the air'.

Anyway, his aeroplanes got so popular that the airfield turned into an airport. Then, years later, the country estate turned into a housing estate. All the streets are named after famous aeroplanes. This sounds like a nice idea, and I admit that Concorde Circus, Spitfire Street and Gulfstream Walk all sound good. It's just a pity that a lot of planes – especially war planes – are named after extreme weather conditions and annoying insects. Hurricane Way, Cyclone Walk and Typhoon Avenue all sound like really windy places to live. The people on Mosquito Street and Wasp Lane are always trying to get the community council to change their names. Then there's all the planes that just have numbers. Try explaining to a pizza-delivery robot that you live in house number 4 on 747 Street. Or number 52 B-52 Street.

We live at number 23 Stealth Street (a kind of bomber plane).

And then there are the robots. There are so many different species of them that Skyways is like a robot petting zoo.

Our pizzas are delivered by Pizzabot – basically an oven on

wheels that says *'Buon appetito!'* when it arrives with your pizza. The streets are cleaned by DustHogs – big hedgehoggy things that wander around all day sucking up leaves and litter through their rubber trunks. There are little DustHog hutches in the base of the solar-powered lamp posts. When their batteries run down, they back themselves into the hutches and recharge. There's even a little DustHog dormitory round the back of the Community Hub where they all go at night after they've discharged their rubbish. Our wheelie bins are robots too. You throw the rubbish in, and they sort it out into recycling and non-recycling.

What do all these robots have in common? They are all really disappointing. Basically just walking, talking furniture.

Eric is *not* a disappointing robot. Eric is the most-not-disappointing robot you could ever meet.

As we flew over the estate, the sun bounced off his big helmet head and his breastplate chest. If you were looking up from one of the front

gardens, we would have looked like a comet flashing by, taking a short cut through the solar system.

But we weren't a comet.

We were me and Eric, and we were taking a short cut to the R–U–Recycling scrapyard . . . and Eric's final destruction.

STEP 6: R-U-RECYCLING

We climbed so high into the sky I could see the river shining on the other side of the airport. The runways stretched out into the grassy hills like fingers pointing to faraway places. Blue mountains rose up on the other side of the river. I thought, *If we keep going up, we'll be in space.* I clung tight to Eric's massive arms.

Then the picture began to come into focus. The green splurge of ground became individual trees. The brick aeroplane of the estate became individual houses. We were coming down. I tried to spot Stealth Street. For a mad moment, I imagined the helicopter setting us down in our back garden. Mum would look through the kitchen window and see a helicopter landing, and then I'd step out and say, 'Surprise!'

But that's not where we were going. We swerved left, heading towards a little tarmac road leading to a place where sunlight sparked off mounds of glass and metal.

The R-U-Recycling scrapyard.

The helicopter's tail lurched back and forth as it

tried to hover in one spot. It wasn't coming down. But we were. They were lowering the metal cable that Eric and I were dangling from.

For the first time in a while, I could hear something louder than helicopter blades.

I looked down.

Beneath my feet was something way more frightening than a sixty-metre drop. Beneath my feet – and getting nearer by the second – was a metal crusher. Huge steel teeth were gnashing at the empty air, getting ready to chew Eric to pieces. And me along with him.

Because no one knew I was there. They thought they were going to destroy a robot. Not a mostly flesh-and-blood kid.

'Eric!' I gasped. 'We're going to be crushed to death!'

Eric tucked up his knees, the way you do when you're going to dive-bomb in the pool.

'Great. Well, that's going to give us an extra one and a half seconds of life.'

I couldn't just hear the noise of the crusher now. I could smell the diesel from its turbines and catch the wind from its exhaust. We were just a few metres from its jaws.

Eric leaned to the left. The cable swung a little. He leaned to the right. It swung a bit more. He rocked from side to side. The cable swung wider and wider. What was he trying to do? I looked up. The helicopter was really struggling. Maybe it would give up and fly us out of danger? Maybe it would crash.

Eric kept rocking and swinging, reaching further and further out. Finally I looked down and saw that we were swinging out over a skip full of tree branches and grass cuttings. We skimmed back across the crusher, into the air on the other side and back across the garden–waste skip. And that's when Eric dropped me.

I landed on a pillow of stinging nettles. But I didn't notice the stings until later. What I noticed was that I was not dead. Because Eric had saved my life.

Eric had saved *my* life, but now he was going to lose his. OK, he doesn't exactly have a *life* because he's a machine – but, if someone saves your life, it doesn't matter what they're made of. You can't just stand back and watch them being crushed into a metal cube.

The sound of the helicopter was getting quieter and quieter. That could only mean they'd dropped Eric and were now flying away. I flung myself over the side of the skip and ran to the crusher. There was a big steel handle with a perished rubber cover, covered in oil. I threw myself at it. I tried to push it up.

The crushing machine spoke: *'Are you sure you want to close down action now? Closing down action will result in metal object not being crushed.'*

'Yes! Stop! Now!'

The machine went slightly quiet, like it was thinking.

There was a sound like it was raining buckets and kettles. It had let go of Eric. He clattered down the feed slide and landed just a metre from me.

My ears were still ringing, but a voice chainsawed through the sound.

'What do you think you're doing?'

A woman with a lot of tattoos and a shiny silver helmet was striding towards me, waving her fist.

'Get away from that thing!' she shouted, pushing back the visor on her helmet. 'No unauthorized persons in this yard. What are you doing here?'

'Oh, you know –' I shrugged – 'I just dropped in.' Which was true after all.

As she got closer, I whispered to Eric, 'Sit really still. I've got a plan that will get us out of here. But you need to sit very still.'

'You just,' growled the woman, 'dropped in?' She made it sound like the most unbelievable thing anyone had ever said. 'Well, you'd better just hop out again. This is a dangerous environment. We're in receipt of an unauthorized robot, which Health and Safety have declared a danger to life and limb.'

'Oh,' I said, 'that's interesting.'

'No, it's not interesting. It's dangerous. Get out of here.'

'OK.' I made as if to leave. 'Before I go . . . see that suit of armour over there?' I pointed to Eric. 'I was wondering if I could take it. For school. We're doing the Wars of the Roses.'

'Rusty!'

I thought she was being rude about Eric's complexion – there are bits of rust on his cheeks – but it turned out to be someone's name: a man with red hair who came running up from somewhere behind the large-domestic-items skip. He was wearing goggles, and on his back there was a yellow gas canister. In his hand, he was carrying a long metal wand. At the end of the wand was a hissing blue flame. He waved the flame around as he trotted towards us.

'This is the best flame I've ever mixed,' he said. 'It will cut through this joker like a hot knife through Nutella. Just you wait and see.'

He bent down over Eric. He was about to start slicing him up! I couldn't look. It was horrible. Rusty pulled up his goggles and looked at Tattoo Woman.

'Would you mind moving its head,' he said. 'I don't like the way it's looking at me. It looks . . . sad.'

Tattoo Woman rolled her eyes. 'Give me the cutter,' she said. 'I'll do it. I don't care if it looks at me or not.'

Rusty sighed. 'OK – I'll try again . . . I've never got the flame this fierce before. I want to try it out.' He pulled down his goggles and stepped closer to Eric.

'NOOOO!' I leaped forward and tried to grab hold of the cutter. It didn't work. I forgot that I wasn't wearing my Osprey. Instead of grabbing the cutter, I just nudged it downwards. Blue flames clawed at Eric's chest, instead of his head.

Rusty jumped back. 'Whoa – what are you doing?'

he roared. 'You could've burned my leg off!'

'But this suit of armour could be of great historical importance,' I said. 'If you destroy it, you could end up in big trouble.'

'It's not a suit of armour. It's an illegal robot.'

'Well, we're doing knights of old in school,' I said, 'and that definitely looks like a suit of armour to me. I could take it away. No charge. Then it won't be cluttering up your yard.'

'It's a robot,' said Rusty. 'It nearly killed a kid at the airport not half an hour ago. Stand well back.'

I've learned that if you keep talking long enough sometimes people just give up. So I started to explain about the Wars of the Roses and what the different parts of a suit of armour are called.

'Nobody cares about the Wars of the Roses!' said Tattoo Woman.

'Controversial,' I said. 'Without the Wars of the Roses—'

'How can it be a suit of armour?' said Rusty. 'It's only got one leg!'

'Maybe it's a suit of armour for a one-legged knight,' I said. 'Not everyone's got loads of legs and feet and hands, you know . . .' As I said this, I lifted my right arm so he could see I had no hand.

Works every time.

Rusty was one hundred per cent embarrassed. 'Of

course,' he said. 'I never thought of that. So. You want this suit of armour? For school? No problem.'

Tattoo Woman was about ninety-three per cent embarrassed. 'You can borrow a SmartTruck to get him to school, if you like. Make sure you send it straight back though.'

I'd never seen a SmartTruck before. It's basically a big adjustable seat on wheels. The smart thing is, you don't have to push it. It synchs with your phone and follows you around. Tattoo Woman slipped the seat under Eric, pressed a few buttons, and it lifted him into place.

'You take him off to your school,' she said. 'The SmartTruck will bring itself back here when you've finished. Good luck. Hope you get top marks.'

I've saved Eric, I thought. Which is when a police car swung in through the scrap yard gates and did not stop until it was dangerously close to us, right on the ramp of the crusher.

An officer wound down the window and called out, 'If I could just ask you to turn your crusher on now and put the target in the machine.'

'What?' said Tattoo Woman.

'The robot. We dropped it into the crusher. Can I just ask you to crush it now.'

'Oh,' she said. 'There's been a mix-up. It's not a robot. It's a suit of armour. From the Wars of the Roses.'

'No mix-up,' said the police officer. 'It's a highly dangerous, unlicensed robot, which almost killed a kid this morning and subsequently kidnapped him.'

'That was me!' I said. 'And I wasn't *that* kidnapped.'

The police officer rolled his eyes.

'Besides,' I said, 'how could it kidnap me? It's just a suit of armour. Of purely historical interest. It doesn't even move, does it?'

I said this a little bit louder than normal, to remind Eric not to move.

Finally, and with an air of menace, the police officer got out of his car. He looked down at me and at Eric and snarled, 'This machine has already caused disruption at the airport. It has distressed the little boy . . .'

I told him that I wasn't distressed, but he just said, 'You THINK you're not distressed now, but you will be later. And you'll be even more distressed if you don't follow the instructions and TURN THE CRUSHER ON.'

That's when I first noticed that Eric is – above all – very eager to please people. Because the moment the police officer said 'turn the crusher on', Eric said:

I AM YOUR OBEDIENT SERVANT.

Eric reached out and pulled the start lever.

Tattoo Woman told me later they normally do ten different safety checks before starting up the crusher.

Eric just pulled the manual override. Thinking about it now, it wasn't Eric who parked the police car on the crusher's lifting ramp, was it? It was the police officer. So, when the crusher hoisted the police officer's car into the air and tilted it towards the mouth of the crusher, that was nothing to do with Eric.

Also, why didn't the police officer do something, instead of standing there watching as his car was tipped into the crusher mumbling, 'No, no, no, no, no' to himself? Did he say or do anything to stop it? No. When the police car lurched off the end of the lift and rolled into the crusher's jaws, did he push Eric aside and try to put the machine into reverse?

Well, not going to lie – he did try. But Eric is hard to push. The back end of the police car buckled. Inside its huge cage, the crusher woke like some terrible beast. The pistons of its stomach punched upwards. The panels of its side moved in and out. Even the police officer couldn't help watching, transfixed. It is quite a spectacle. Especially at the end when everything goes very, very quiet, and then there's one last absolutely deafening *CLANG*.

A panel opened and, instead of a police car, one beautifully perfect cube of metal about the size of a washing machine slid down the chute. The officer looked down at it. You could still make out the 'P' of Police on one of its sides.

That, I thought, is definitely controversial.

'Why did you do that?' sobbed the police officer.

I'M SORRY, I CAN'T ANSWER THAT QUESTION.

STEP 7: CONTROVERSIAL

The police officer stared at the metal block. Tattoo Woman placed her hand on his shoulder. Rusty didn't seem to know what to do, so he turned off the flame cutter out of respect.

'What am I going to tell them at HQ?' said the police officer.

'Tell them you can't remember where you parked your squad car. Tell them it was stolen.'

'Or tell them it was squashed by a giant robot.'

While they were coming up with explanations, I walked slowly back towards the exit.

The SmartTruck, with Eric sitting in it, followed me. Its electric engine was silent as a smile.

Out on the road, the bus was coming. If I could just get Eric on board and get out of there, we'd be OK. But the bus had other ideas.

The doors hissed open. I tapped my travel card on the card reader and requested the access ramp. As the ramp slid down, the bus spoke. *'Unexpectedly heavy weight on the access ramp,'* it said.

Mum says that back when the buses had drivers you knew who to speak to if there was a problem. When the bus speaks now, the voice just comes at you like God on High is talking. You don't even know where to look.

So I said, 'It's lost property,' to the air.

Which probably would have been a good explanation, if Eric hadn't said:

I AM ERIC. HOW DO YOU DO, AND WHO ARE YOU?

'*Unexpectedly heavy item speaks*,' said the bus. '*Please pay full fare.*'

'Are you saying that if a thing speaks, it must be a person? What about you? You speak. You're not a person. You're a bus.'

This was probably not the right thing to say. It seemed to be news to the bus that it wasn't a person. It switched its engine off. It went very quiet.

I looked back down the road to see if the police were coming. We had to get out of here fast. We got on the bus.

The only other passenger was an old lady who was shouting jokes at her grandchildren on FaceTime. She looked up for a second when the engine went off, but then went back to her phone.

I KNOW HUNDREDS OF AMUSING JOKES AND FACTS.

'*Lost property knows jokes*,' said the bus.

'So now if you know stuff, you're a person. Is that what you're saying?'

'*Full fare, please.*'

'My phone knows nearly everything, AND it can talk. Are you going to charge my phone full fare?'

'*Philosophy*,' said the bus, as if it was thinking all this over.

There was still no sign of the police officer. I suppose he was busy trying to explain how his car ended up as a small metal cube.

Then the bus said, '*Philosophy is causing delays to the service. Please sit down. End philosophy.*' The engine started up again.

Eric tried to get up, but I told him not to.

'Stay in the SmartTruck until I find your missing leg,' I said.

The SmartTruck followed me down the aisle and backed itself into the wheelchair space.

'Remember, the police are after you,' I whispered. 'Try not to attract attention. Just sit there and be boring.'

The old lady looked up from her phone and stared at Eric. He tipped his head towards her and said:

I AM AT YOUR SERVICE.

I smiled at her. She stared at Eric. I thought I'd better explain.

'Suit of armour,' I said. 'School project.' Then I whispered to Eric, 'Just sit tight. We'll be on the estate in a few minutes.'

I AM LOOKING FORWARD TO BEING OF SERVICE TO YOU, SIR, ON YOUR ESTATE.

'Yes,' I said, looking out of the window. 'We're just arriving on the estate now.'

Eric looked out at the rows of little houses with neat lawns and big windows. I somehow don't think Skyways was the kind of estate he had in mind.

The woman squinted at Eric. 'Is that suit of armour talking?' she said.

'My friend,' I explained, 'is inside. It's for a play. About the Wars of the Roses.' I checked the app on my phone to see if I could figure out where my hand was.

Eric seemed to think this meant he ought to carry on the conversation with the old woman.

I CAN ALSO ASSIST AT SHOOTING PARTIES.

'Shooting parties?'

SHOOTING PARTIES ON YOUR SHOOTING ESTATE.

'Shooting? On the estate?' gasped the woman.

I AM ABLE TO CLEAN AND LOAD GUNS.

'He means historical guns. From history,' I said.

'You want to get your facts straight,' said the old lady. 'They didn't have guns during the Wars of the Roses.'

'Actually,' I said, 'fire arms known as arquebuses were used at Bosworth Field, the last battle of the Wars of the Roses.'

Is it weird, by the way, that I could remember the Wars of the Roses but not my own accident?

'I stand corrected,' said the old lady. 'It's a very impressive suit of armour. Can I get a selfie?'

'No,' I said, a bit too quickly. 'Please. We don't want anyone to steal our idea. We'd really appreciate it if you kept this to yourself.'

'It cheers my heart,' said the

old lady, 'to see a young person make such an effort with their education.'

When she said that, a memory was triggered. This happens to me sometimes. I can see something I'd forgotten all about, playing like a YouTube clip in my head.

This time, it was school, back when we really were doing Wars of the Roses and making cereal-packet castles. I could see the faces of friends I'd forgotten: Christian Walker, who never stopped talking; his brother Benedict, who never stopped telling him to shut up; Agnes, who was always crazy early. I'd hardly seen any of them since I started at the Limb Lab. But one day soon I'd be back at school, and maybe on the first day they'd be like, 'Hey, Alfie – what've you been doing?' And I'd say, 'I'll show you. Come in, Eric.' And in would walk my gigantic mechanical knight . . .

I was still daydreaming when we got to Stealth Street. I always have to stand on tip-toes to get the facial-recognition lock to open the front door. Then it says, '*Good afternoon* –' pause while it scans your face – '*ALFIE!*'

It always shouts my name like I'm the last person it's expecting to see. Even though there are only two of us living in the house, and it sees me every day.

The door clicked open and said, '*Please go through.*'

I AM YOUR OBEDIENT SERVANT, said Eric.

And then he did go through. Right through the door. He put his one massive foot against it and pushed it clean off its hinges. Like I said, Eric has a tendency to take things a bit literally. The door see-sawed down on to the step, and got wedged in the entrance, making the perfect ramp for the SmartTruck to zoom up and into the house.

'That,' I said, 'is definitely going to be controversial.'

STEP 8: UNLEASH YOUR POWERS

You know when you get a new phone or something, and you just want to rip the box open right there in the shop, and you're so excited that you don't even read the instructions?

That's what I was like when I got Eric home. I didn't even CARE that the front door was broken. I just wanted to get him inside and see what he could do. He looked like the kind of robot that could shoot lasers from its eyes. Or bullets from its fingers. Or could transform into a fast car. Or a rocket.

And he was my obedient servant.

'OK, Eric,' I said. 'Unleash your powers!'

There was a long pause. A whirr of cogs. A mechanical brain was thinking. Then . . .

SORRY. I DO NOT COMPREHEND.

'You're my obedient servant. Show me what you can do.'

I AM ERIC. I AM LOST.

'Not any more, because I found you. What can you actually do?'

I CAN PERFORM A RANGE OF HOUSEHOLD CHORES. SUGGESTIONS: FLOORS – SWEEPING OF; CLOTHES – IRONING OF.

Ironing? . . . Clothes?

I thought I'd found Iron Man. I'd actually found Ironing Man.

I CAN WELCOME GUESTS.

'We never have any guests.'

ANSWER THE TELEPHONE.

'Nobody answers the telephone any more.'

I CAN POLISH SILVER.

'Silver? What kind of silver?'

I CAN ALSO PREPARE A LIGHT SNACK.

If you've been hoping for laser-firing lessons, a snack is definitely a disappointment. But it is a snack.

I CAN PREPARE CUCUMBER SAND-WICHES.

'Cucumber sandwiches are not a snack. Cucumber sandwiches are just a way of hiding cucumber.'

EGGS.

Eggs could be good, I thought. So I filled a pan full of water and handed him a couple of eggs.

Eric's approach to eggs was different, to say the least. He closed his fingers, crushing the eggs into his steel palm. Then opened his palm again. His hand was glowing red hot.

He literally grilled the eggs on his own hand. They sizzled. They bubbled. The bits of broken shell inside them glowed white with heat.

The heat from Eric's hand blasted my face. I had to screw up my eyes. Which was just as well because soon the little bits of broken shell started flying around the room like tiny hot bullets.

I WILL COOK FOR THREE MINUTES OR TO TASTE.

'No! No! Stop! You're going to burn the place down! We're being shelled by eggs.'

Eric nodded, and then turned his hand round so the palm was pointing down. Incinerated egg flopped on to the floor, black and bubbly like a deep-fried bat.

It was not food.

But it was excellent.

I said, 'Do it again!' and gave him two more eggs.

One of the shells filled up with hot air, and then exploded like a hand grenade.

They were the last two eggs, so I thought I'd see how he was with toast.

Slices of bread caught fire within five seconds.

The wrapper of the loaf lit up, swelled up into a blazing ball of fire, and floated around the room like a little lost dragon.

I also tried him with raisins: they squeal, then hiss, then suddenly fossilize.

Cheese: goes gooey at first, then flows like hot lava on to the floor.

Sugar: smells like all the sweets you ever wanted, but then turns into evil superglue.

Salt: blazes blue!

Plastic: don't. Smells like poo.

Very thinly sliced potato: I thought this might lead to crisps. And it did! I sprinkled some of them with salt and doused them with vinegar, but when I tried to eat some, Eric put his hand up to stop me. He poured the crisps into one of Mum's best bowls and gave them to me on a tray.

He really is a polite robot, I thought, as I sat there munching my way through a massive bowl of salt-and-vinegar crisps. OK, I may not have a laser-blasting war-bot, but I do seem to have a massive crisp-making machine.

Then the DustUrchin came scuttling in. Dust-Urchins are the baby version of the DustHogs we have patrolling the streets. They have little spikes on their backs to make them look cute. When their batteries run down, just like the bigger versions, they back themselves into little recharging hutches.

As robots go, they are among the more disappointing robots.

Now, our DustUrchin parked itself at Eric's feet. It doesn't have eyes – just a couple of lights on its front bumper. But if you looked at it now you would swear it was staring up at Eric.

Have you ever seen when two babies meet?

They don't talk because they can't talk. But they always check each other out.

Eric: *Stares at DustUrchin*

DustUrchin: *Stares at Eric* *'Today is September twenty-third,'* it says.

Eric seemed to think this was the DustUrchin's way of introducing itself.

I AM ERIC. YOUR OBEDIENT SERVANT.

The DustUrchin's headlights flickered. It was

obviously happy to have found a new friend.

'*You have one local news update,*' it said. '*Police today are looking for a large humanoid robot, which caused some disruption at the airport and damage to police property. The weather is slightly overcast with sunny intervals and a five per cent chance of rain. Have a great day.*'

'Wait,' I said. 'The police? What was that about the police?'

I'd just been having so much fun with Eric that I'd totally forgotten there would be consequences.

'*You have ONE phone message,*' said the DustUrchin, ignoring my panic.

I didn't even know until then that the DustUrchin sucked up phone messages as well as dust.

'*Hi, Alfie,*' it said in a voice that was definitely my mum's but also quite robotty, as though it had vacuumed up Mum, and she was trapped inside it. '*Home in fifteen. Tell the kettle!*'

Fifteen minutes!

The floor of the kitchen was crusted with tiny stalagmites of blasted sugar and puddled with melted cheese.

The front door was lying on its side in the hallway.

And, worst of all, there was a gigantic fugitive robot in the kitchen.

I CAN PERFORM SMALL HOUSEHOLD REPAIRS.

'Can you? Can you honestly? Can you put the door back?'

Eric picked up the door as easily as if it had been made of tissue paper. We propped it back into place. The middle finger of his left hand turned out to be a screwdriver.

I said, 'Oh! Snap! I've got a screwdriver too. Though mine's in my thumb.'

Eric fixed the door. The DustUrchin fixed the kitchen. Its trunk sucked up the crumbs, sugar and incinerated egg. It even wormed its way up the wall to unexpected heights cleaning the tiles and the pipes.

In ten minutes, the kitchen looked so clean you would never know that a giant robot had heated a tonne of ingredients to the point of nuclear meltdown.

'You've saved my life,' I said to the DustUrchin.

If Mum had seen the mess, she would have been completely triggered.

She also would not have been thrilled to hear we were sheltering a fugitive from justice in the house – even if it was made of metal. I had to find some way of hiding Eric.

Then I heard the house say, *'Welcome home, Mrs Miles. Do go through . . .'* and the front door swing open.

'Ow!' That was Mum. 'What's going on?'

'What do you mean?'

'The front door just opened outwards. Hit me in the shoulder.'

'Doesn't it always open outwards?' I was hoping the malfunctioning door would distract her long enough for me to get Eric out of sight.

'No. It always opens inwards.'

'Are you sure?' I said, still playing for time.

I managed to get Eric into the corner of the kitchen.

'Stay there and be quiet,' I hissed.

I AM YOUR OBEDIENT SERVANT.

'What?' said Mum.

'Nothing. I just said are you sure it opened inwards before?'

'All front doors open inwards.'

'All? Really?' I managed to click the kitchen door shut behind me. If I could just keep her out until I could get rid of Eric . . .

'I'm a postwoman, Alfie. I do front doors for a living.'

'And I bet you have done more than enough doors today, so don't go near the kitchen door. Go and have a nice sit-down, and I'll make you a cup of tea.'

'I have to admit,' said Mum, 'that is the best offer I've had all day.'

She settled down in the big chair, and I took her over a cup of tea and what was left of the bowl of crisps.

'Where did you get these, Alfie?'

'Made them.'

'Made them? From potatoes?'

'Potatoes, yeah.'

'That you chopped with your own hand?'

'Well . . .' In all the excitement of test-driving Eric, I had forgotten that I had lost my Osprey. 'What do you think?' I asked, a bit too quickly, hiding my arms behind my back. 'Crispy enough?'

She took a handful. Between crunches, she said, 'What else is cooking?'

I didn't know what she was on about.

'I hear the sound of pan lids rattling,' she said.

I could hear that too. I knew it wasn't pan lids, though. It was the sound of Eric's metal joints clinking as he tried to get comfortable behind the kitchen door.

'It's a surprise!' I said, dashing out into the kitchen. I turned the radio on to cover the sound. This was a mistake. Every station seemed to be playing a song with a question in it. And Eric tried to answer every question.

'Should I stay or should I go . . . ?'

I DON'T HAVE ENOUGH INFORMATION TO ANSWER THAT QUESTION.

'Where is the love . . . ?'

IF YOU HAVE LOST SOMETHING, TRY RETRACING YOUR STEPS.

I turned the radio off.

81

'Who are you talking to? I can hear voices in there.'

'Oh,' I called, 'just the robot.' This was the truth. But I knew she'd think I was talking about the DustUrchin.

'Oh. Where is that little fella?' she cooed.

I heard the DustUrchin scuttle over, suck up the rubbish, and mention that it was a lovely day with only a five per cent chance of rain. *'Police are continuing to search,'* it said, *'for the runaway robot.'*

Now my brain was buffering. Should I make more tea or smuggle Eric out?

I CAN PREPARE LIGHT SNACKS, said Eric, as if he'd been reading my mind.

'Oh!' I said. 'That's brilliant. Yes. Do you know any recipes easy enough for me to cook? No exploding eggshells.'

WHY NOT TRY CLASSIC WELSH RABBIT?

'We haven't got any rabbits, Eric.'

It turns out that Welsh rabbit is also called Welsh rarebit and is nothing to do with real rabbits.

ERIC'S RECIPE FOR WELSH RABBIT, said Eric.

1. **PUT SOME CHEESE, BUTTER, WORCESTERSHIRE SAUCE, MUSTARD, FLOUR AND PEPPER IN A PAN WITH SOME MILK.**
2. **HEAT UP YOUR FINGER.**

3. STIR THE MIXTURE WITH YOUR HOT FINGER UNTIL IT IS A THICK PASTE.
4. PLACE A SLICE OF BREAD ON THE PALM OF YOUR HAND.
5. HEAT UP YOUR HAND UNTIL THE BREAD IS TOASTED ON ONE SIDE.
6. SPREAD THE RABBIT PASTE OVER THE UNTOASTED SIDE ON A PLATE.
7. HOLD YOUR HOT HAND OVER THIS UNTIL THE MIXTURE STARTS TO BUBBLE AND GO BROWN.

'What's going on in there?' called Mum.

'Don't come in! Just relax!'

I did everything Eric said, only using the cooker and the grill instead of electric hands. It's not easy to use a cheese grater with one hand. And the pieces of Welsh rarebit were a bit uneven. As I was about to take them through to the living room, Eric popped a pair of napkins on to two plates. We don't normally have napkins at all. And these napkins were folded into the shape of swans.

'Where did you learn to do that?' said Mum.

'In dexterity class.'

'You're working so hard to be the best you can be,' she said. 'You've got a world-class state-of-the-art hand. There's no telling what you'll be able to achieve if you just keep working at it. Now, shall we watch this nice documentary about Genghis Khan?'

So we ate our Welsh rarebits and watched actors recreating massacres and bloodbaths all over medieval Mongolia.

'He was a bad lot, old Genghis,' said Mum, making it sound like she had known him since he was in nappies. 'But, you've got to admit, he really knew how to organize a postal service. Relay stations with fresh horses and hot food all over the empire. A letter could get from one end of the Silk Road to the other in a week. Amazing.' She does tend to relate everything to the postal service. 'This is very good Welsh rarebit, by the way. I'll do the washing-up.'

Sitting with Mum watching Mongol hordes burn cities and massacre people was so cosy and relaxing that I completely forgot that the whole snack thing was just a trick to keep her out of the kitchen.

'No, no – I'll wash up.'

'Cook doesn't wash up. It's the rules. Besides, you're not wearing your hand.'

So she'd noticed. I thought I'd got away with it. Mum notices everything. She also asks the most awkward questions.

'Where is it, Alfie?'

'It's being adjusted,' I said, trying not to tell an actual lie, because one of the things she definitely notices is lies. 'I'll be wearing it again tomorrow.' I smiled reassuringly as I took Mum's plate from her hand and made my way to the kitchen.

It's not easy to hide a massive robot.

It's not like you can tuck him into a cupboard.

I closed the door that led back to the living room and opened the door that led to the bedrooms and bathroom. I ran the kitchen taps at full pelt, put the kettle on to make as much noise as possible, and shuffled Eric back on to the SmartTruck. Right then, I was so glad our house had no stairs. I led the truck out of the kitchen and into the bedroom corridor. Past my room. Past Mum's. Up to the door at the end, on the other side of the bathroom – the door that's always closed. I had to shove it hard to get it to budge.

ALLOW ME.

'No! No more door destruction.'

I finally pushed the door open, waved Eric through, and shut it after him.

I stood still in the corridor. Do you ever have those moments when you think you're about to sneeze? It's like that for me when I feel like I'm on the brink of remembering something important. I froze outside the door with a memory fluttering in the corner of my mind.

Then it flew away again.

'So,' said Mum as I walked back into the living room, 'what's going on?'

I stopped in my tracks.

How much did she know? About the airport? About Eric? It could be anything. Mum is like human Facebook. She knows when everyone's birthday is – because she delivers their cards. If you're old and you can't get out, she'll tell you all the news and gossip. And people tell her news too.

She gestured around. 'Why is everywhere so clean and tidy?'

'Because I cleaned and tidied.'

'Why did you clean and tidy?'

'Just thought it would be nice.'

'It must have taken ages. You must have started the moment you got back from Limb Lab.'

I didn't say anything.

'You did go to Limb Lab, didn't you, Alfie?'

'Of course I did. You saw the napkins.'

'Good boy. Come on. Give me a hug.'

It's not that easy to do a one-handed hug. It can come out more like some desperate wrestling move.

'Maybe it's easier,' she said, 'if I give *you* a hug.' Which she did. 'Alfie, you've got all your life ahead of you. Get out there and live it. Like Genghis. Only not like Genghis. You know what they say – smart gets smarter.' Mum is always telling me what they say, but never explains who 'they' are.

*

Our house dims the lights and switches off all screens at 10 p.m. *'Good sleep hygiene,'* it says, *'makes good health.'* If you want to look something up on your phone, you've got to get right under the duvet where the house can't see you.

As soon as I was in bed, I was straight on the HandShake app, looking for some sign of my hand, trying to figure out where it was. It told me it still had three fingers of battery, so that was something. But it gave its location as on a motorway heading north.

What could I do? What's the point of an app that tells you where something is but doesn't tell you how to get it back? If I could only operate the hand by remote control, I could maybe turn the car round.

I had no idea what to do or how to explain how I had come to lose my state-of-the-art hand. I couldn't sleep. So, instead, I tried finding out more about Eric. Who made him? When? What for? Who did he belong to? If I could find out where he came from, then maybe I could take him back there. Maybe there would be a vast reward.

I scrolled through every page looking for stuff about Eric the Robot. There was a lot about various other Erics, such as Eric the Red, Eric the Angry, Eric the First, Eric the Second, and so on. The middle name of most Erics seems to be 'the'.

There was also a lot about every kind of robot:

mobile and immobile, soft and hard, independent, remote-controlled, industrial, recreational, robots the size of postal districts that could cut tunnels through rock, robots the size of molecules that could move through your bloodstream, robots the size of little bees that can swarm, robots you could send into space . . .

There was some stuff about the first ever robot – which was built by St Albert the Great. He called it an android. One of his pupils smashed it because it wouldn't stop talking. And I was distracted for a while by the Leonardo da Vinci robot, which is the double of Eric. Honestly, look it up. It's basically a suit of armour with an engine in it.

But although there was loads about robots and about loads of different Erics, there was nothing about Eric the Robot.

Unless I'd found an original Leonardo da Vinci in Lost Property . . . What if Eric was a lost masterpiece? I could polish him up and sell him to a museum for a fortune.

I curled up and let the relaxing thoughts of fame and fortune lull me to sleep.

STEP 9: THE EMERGENCY HAIRBRUSH

Postwomen start work early.

The house turns on Mum's bedside lamp at 5 a.m. and makes her a cup of tea at 5.15 a.m. By 5.30 a.m., she's out of the front door, and I'm in my school uniform. As soon as I hear the front door click shut, I go to get Eric out of his hiding place.

As soon as I opened the door to the room, I had that almost-remembering feeling again. But Eric tried to stand up, and I forgot about everything apart from the danger of being crushed by a falling robot.

'Sit down,' I said. 'The truck will bring you out of there.'

WOULD YOU LIKE A MORNING PAPER, SIR? I COULD IRON IT FOR YOU.

'Iron a paper? What for?'

I'M SORRY. I CAN'T ANSWER THAT QUESTION.

'Why would anyone want an ironed newspaper?' It seems that Eric was the robot of useless skills.

I synched my phone with the SmartTruck, and it

followed me with Eric into the kitchen.

In the morning light, I could see patches of rust on his chest. I found a packet of oven-cleaning pads at the back of the kitchen cupboard. They foamed up like soap when I rubbed them on his rusty neck and back and elbows. When I scrubbed his back, he leaned forward helpfully. When I scrubbed under his arms, he held his arms up.

'You are loving this, aren't you, Eric?' I said. 'You love a good scrub.'

He didn't answer, but he did *look* as though he was loving it. He leaned way back on his chair as if he were wallowing in a warm bath.

Good thing about being at the Limb Lab is that if you don't turn up they just assume you've gone to school. And if you don't go to school they assume you're at the Limb Lab.

So no one is looking for you.

I could just keep going until Eric shone all over.

I picked up a can of WD-40 Eric lifted up his arms, as if he wanted me to spray some of the oil into his armpits like deodorant.

'There you go, Eric. Looking a bit smarter now.'

SMARTER . . .

Eric raised his hand and fanned his fingers out in front of me. They were glowing red-hot. Steam drifted from the gaps in his knuckles.

'What are you doing?'

It was not relaxing, feeling the heat from his fingers in my face. He reached over and pinched my sleeves.

'Eric, you could burn me. Let go.'

But he ran his fingers up and down, leaving the sleeves with a perfectly ironed crease.

You may think that a robot that does the ironing is a boring idea. That's because no one has ever ironed your clothes WHILE YOU WERE WEARING THEM.

It's not boring.

It's terrifying.

He ironed my collar with my neck still inside it. When he started on my trousers, I was sure I was going to end up as the smoky bit of a buttock barbecue. But no. I just ended up as someone with very smart trousers.

Eric didn't think I looked sharp enough, though.

A GENTLEMAN'S SOCKS, he said, **SHOULD ALWAYS MATCH THE COLOUR OF HIS TROUSERS.**

'I admit they're very red,' I said. 'But I love my LFC socks. They're just so fleecy inside.'

IT IS SOMETIMES PERMISSIBLE FOR A GENTLEMAN'S SOCKS TO MATCH HIS TIE INSTEAD OF HIS TROUSERS.

'I'm not wearing a tie.'

EXACTLY SO.

'I'm not only not wearing a tie,' I said. 'I don't even own one.'

A GENTLEMAN SHOULD ALWAYS WEAR A TIE. ALLOW ME, SIR.

He opened his emergency panel and pulled out a drawer. If you asked me what you might need in an emergency, I'd have said fire extinguisher and distress flare, but Eric's emergency drawer was full of rolled-up old-fashioned ties, cufflinks, a toothbrush and a hairbrush. Apparently Eric thought the best thing to do in an emergency was smarten up.

IF YOU'LL PERMIT ME, SIR, said Eric. He flipped up the collar of my shirt.

'No,' I said. 'I don't permit you.'

I don't know if you've ever tried Not Permitting a six-foot-six man of steel to do something? It's not easy. Eric put a red tie round my neck and waited while I tried to figure out how to tie it.

VERY SATISFACTORY, SIR.

I checked myself in the mirror, but Eric started brushing my hair with his emergency hairbrush.

I said, 'Get off! You're supposed to be my obedient servant.'

A GENTLEMAN LOOKS HIS BEST AT ALL TIMES, SIR. WHEN A GENTLEMAN IS WEARING A TIE, HE SHOULD ALSO WEAR A JACKET.

'What? You MADE me wear the tie. I'll take it off again.'

NOT UNTIL AFTER DINNER, SIR. DO YOU HAVE A JACKET, SIR?

'NO, I don't have a jacket.'

Eric didn't say anything, but he started to rattle. If robots do have feelings, then that rattling is probably the sound of robot sadness. The nearest thing I have to a jacket is my old school blazer, so I went and got it.

VERY SMART, SIR. His eyes glowed soft blue.

After that, he wanted to polish my shoes. Except I was wearing trainers. I explained that you can't polish trainers. After that, I had to explain what trainers were. Then he explained that trainers were not acceptable footwear. He explained this so loudly and for so long that, in the end, I got my school shoes and let him polish them. And – just to keep him off my case – I brought in a big basket of washing for him to iron. It was full – not just of T-shirts and trousers, but duvet covers, pillowcases . . . Stuff that takes ages to iron.

He had the whole lot done and folded in minutes.

I'd meant to smarten Eric up, but instead he'd smartened me up.

The DustUrchin peeped out from behind the kitchen door. It snuffled up to Eric, stretched out its rubbery nose and touched Eric's foot. '*The outlook today,*' it said, '*is mostly sunny with a fifteen per cent chance of rain. You have ONE message . . .*'

That robot version of Mum's voice said, '*Morning, sunshine. Have a good day.*' After that, it was the news update: '*The authorities are still searching the Skyways estate for the unlicensed robot that caused damage to police property and disruption at the airport yesterday. Seen a large fugitive robot? Please take a photo and tag it with the words "Rogue Robot".*'

Did Eric understand what the DustUrchin was saying?

Was he worried that the authorities were after him?

You might think robots can't worry. You might be right. All I'm saying is that as soon as Eric heard the words 'authorities are still searching', he sat up really, really straight and said . . .

WHEN DID THE SEA MONSTER EAT THE SHIP?

WHEN IT WAS HUNGRY . . .

Which sounded to me like a joke that had gone wrong.

EXCUSE ME, THAT JOKE WAS INCORRECTLY SPOKEN.

I said to him, 'Eric, don't worry. I'm not going to let the authorities get you. You're possibly a lost Leonardo Da Vinci. You're definitely a fine piece of machinery. You're a mystery, and I'm going to keep you safely hidden away until you're solved.'

Then there was a draught, like the front door had opened, and the house said, *'Welcome. Do come in.'*

Who was coming in? The house only lets people in if it recognizes them. Was it Mum back early from work?

But then the house said the name of probably the worst person to come and visit you when you're trying to hide a large robot.

'*Come in,*' it said. '*Go through, Dr Shilling.*'

I dived out into the hall, parking myself in the doorway so that she wouldn't be able to get past and discover Eric in the kitchen.

Dr Shilling was standing with her hands behind her back. 'Alfie Miles,' she said with a smile. 'I wondered if you needed a hand?'

Before I could think of what to say, she took the Osprey Grip MM out from behind her back and held it out to me.

'Oh! You found it!' Not going to lie, I was more than slightly relieved to see it again. So relieved, in fact, that before I could stop myself, I said, 'Where did you find it?'

Considering I'd lost it at the airport, when I was supposed to be at the Limb Lab, posing a question like that was asking for trouble.

'Interesting question,' said Dr Shilling.

If you didn't know Dr Shilling, you'd probably think the phrase 'interesting question' meant that the question you'd asked was interesting. If you did know her, though, you'd realize that 'interesting question' really means, 'I'm about to start talking, and I won't be stopping any time soon.'

'You left it in the airport,' she said. 'Yesterday. When you were supposed to be at the Limb Lab.'

'Oh. Yes,' I said. 'The airport.'

'Were you meeting someone?'

'Yes. I met someone,' I said. Which was true, because I'd met Eric.

'Well, a lady picked it up there and brought it to the Limb Lab, so I thought I'd bring it straight over.'

'Thank you VERY much,' I said, hoping that she might take that to mean 'goodbye'.

But no. She looked me up and down and said, 'You're looking unusually smart today.'

'Well, you know.' I shrugged. 'Going to the airport.'

'I thought that was yesterday?'

'Yes, that's right. Anyway, thank you.'

I said 'thank you' in a way that I hoped sounded like 'goodbye', but it didn't work. She leaned into the doorway, which meant she was looking straight into the room where Eric was. If she saw Eric, well, things would get properly interesting. I couldn't just shut the door in her face, could I? So I did the only thing I could think of. I dodged past her and stood outside on the pavement so that she had to turn her back on Eric to carry on talking to me. It probably made it look like I had lost my mind.

'I was telling you about this lady,' said Dr Shilling, following me to the kerb. 'She got into her car, threw your hand on the back seat, and her satnav brought her straight to the Limb Lab. The short-range homing device in your hand overrode everything the lady tried to do. So interesting! Your hand was backseat driving.'

GOD SAVE OUR GRACIOUS KING!

Inside the house, Eric's voice was cranking out the national anthem. Blue light from his eyes flickered across the blinds.

'Well . . . it's back now. Thanks very much.'

'Aren't you going to put your hand back on?'

I tried to go back indoors. But then a little red van pulled up.

Mum was home for lunch. I must have been cleaning Eric all morning.

'Dr Shilling! Nice to see you.' Mum spotted my hand. 'Alfie did say you'd been working on his hand.'

'Yes, and now Alfie and his hand have been successfully reunited.'

'Reunited?'

'Dr Shilling was just explaining,' I said, 'my hand's amazing short-range homing device.'

'It's called HandShake,' said Dr Shilling.

I said, 'Can we show Mum how it works? How about I go inside the house, and let's see if it can find me.'

Honestly, from the expression on Dr Shilling's face, you would think I'd said, 'Guess what? It's Christmas morning!' She glowed like fairy lights she was so happy.

'Are you sure you've got enough battery?' she asked,

as if she couldn't believe her luck.

I glanced at my phone. 'Two fingers,' I said, running to the front door while she put my hand down on the pavement.

'I love this,' she said to Mum. 'Count to ten, Alfie! Like in hide-and-seek!'

'Oh, great idea!'

I didn't look back, but I almost felt Mum's eyes narrowing as she tried to figure out what I was up to. OK, she was bound to find out about the airport at some point, but hopefully not until I'd got Eric safely out of the back door.

I crashed into the kitchen where Eric was sitting up in the SmartTruck, still singing the national anthem.

Outside, a too-excited Dr Shilling yelled, 'He's coming – ready or not!'

I dashed through the house and shoved Eric into the yard. 'Eric,' I said, 'if you're going to live life on the run, you're going to need a new leg.'

Back inside, the Osprey hand was on the doorstep. The way HandShake works is that the hand picks up your phone's location, then – well, this is creepy – it crawls towards you. It spreads its fingers on the floor, then bunches them up again so that it shuffles forward. Within seconds, it was clambering over the doorstep and spider crawling down the hallway towards me.

Not going to lie, watching your own hand crawl

towards you across the carpet is an unusual experience. I was mesmerized.

'You've got to admit,' said Dr Shilling from the doorway, 'it's pretty handy.'

I remembered to laugh at this joke.

'Thank you for bringing it back home, Doctor,' said Mum.

'No trouble.'

'Goodbye.'

I bent down to pick up my hand. I really thought I'd got away with it. Then Mum said, 'Oh, Dr Shilling . . . where was Alfie's hand found exactly?'

Slowly Mum closed the front door, never taking her eyes off me.

'The airport,' she said.

It was the last thing she said in a normal voice for a long time. After Dr Shilling left, everything was in capitals . . .

'THE AIRPORT! HOW DID YOUR HAND END UP AT THE AIRPORT?'

'It just fell off. Sort of.'

'AND YOU DIDN'T NOTICE? HOW COULD YOU POSSIBLY NOT NOTICE THAT YOUR HAND HAD COME OFF?'

That was actually an interesting question.

'I SPEND ALL MY TIME WORRYING

ABOUT YOU. AND WORKING ALL HOURS SO THAT WE CAN BE COMFORTABLE, AND IT TURNS OUT YOU ARE JETTING OFF ON HOLIDAY WHILE MY BACK IS TURNED.'

'I didn't get on a plane.'

'OH, WELL – THANK YOU. THANK YOU FOR NOT GOING TO CARACAS. YOU'RE NOT READY TO GO BACK TO SCHOOL, BUT YOU'RE COMPLETELY HAPPY TO CONSIDER INTERNATIONAL TRAVEL.'

'I was just a bit lonely.'

'LONELY! SO YOU WENT TO AN AIRPORT. ANYONE ELSE WOULD GO TO THE LIBRARY. OR THE SHOPS. BUT NO – YOU HAD TO GO TO THE AIRPORT! YOU WERE SUPPOSED TO GO TO THE LIMB LAB!'

'I know, but . . .'

'GIVE ME A HUG!'

What?

This is the thing with people. They are so unpredictable. Not like robots. One minute, Mum was yelling at me furiously. The next, she was giving me a hug.

'I know you've been lonely,' she said. Then she stepped back and looked me up and down. 'You're in your school uniform,' she said. 'Were you thinking of going to school instead of the Limb Lab?'

'I was just, you know, seeing if it still fitted.'

'You look very smart.'

'Thanks.'

'You've even got a tie on. And it's not a tie I recognize. Where did you get that tie?'

'Oh. I was tidying up, and I just found it, so I thought . . .'

When I said 'tidying up' she stopped listening and sniffed. 'I wondered what that smell was. It's the smell of clean.' She spotted the basket of neatly folded ironing. 'You've done all the ironing,' she said.

'Yeah.'

She stood way back and nodded her head. 'My brave boy,' she said. 'You know, I think you are ready.'

'NO! No, I'm really not! I really was just checking.'

'Well, it's good that you're thinking about it. Good that you're trying. Keep trying, Alfie, and we'll get there. But no more airports, eh?'

'No. Sorry about that.'

'And you make sure you go to Limb Lab tomorrow.'

'It's Dexterity Workshop again tomorrow.'

'Exactly.'

'Dexterity is so embarrassing.'

'It won't be. Once you get a bit of dexterity.'

On the way to bed that night, I tried to go back into the room where I'd hidden Eric the night before. I wanted to know what I'd almost remembered in there. I put my hand on the handle, but my brain couldn't seem to make my fingers close round it. I was still trying when Mum came out of the bathroom, brushing her teeth.

She didn't ask me what I was doing, just asked if I was OK. I said, 'Yeah.' She kept staring at me as if she was waiting for me to open the door. So I just said 'Goodnight' and went to bed.

STEP 10: DEXTERITY WORKSHOP

You probably don't know what Dexterity Workshop is. It's the lessons they give us in the Limb Lab on how to deal with the practical and emotional difficulties of having hi-tech body parts.

In other words, Dexterity Workshop is The Worst.

Because everyone else is bursting with dexterity, and I don't have any.

But if I wanted to stay out of trouble in the short term, I needed to go to Dexterity. I also needed to find a way to fix Eric.

The most obvious way to find his missing leg was to get him to try to think where it could be. So, that morning, as I moved him out of the shed, I said to him, 'Eric, your leg – where did you last have it?'

I CANNOT ANSWER THAT QUESTION.

'Try to remember when you first noticed your leg was missing.'

I AM YOUR OBEDIENT SERVANT.

'Exactly. So, obediently, tell me where you were when your leg fell off.'

I WAS LOST.

'Come on. Try. How can anyone not remember what they did with their own left leg?'

Did he glance down at my right hand when I said that? Something made me look at it.

'Look, I'm sorry. It just would be so useful to find your leg.'

WHY DID THE SEA MONSTER EAT THE FISH?

'We don't need jokes. We need your leg.'

I AM SORRY. THAT JOKE WAS INCORRECT.

I know I'd promised Mum I wouldn't go to the airport again, but surely the best place to look for Eric's leg was the place where I'd found the rest of him: Lost Property.

I caught the early bus to the airport. Since my run-in with Happy to Help, I wasn't as casual about blending in as I used to be. I waited for a school group to come through, then tagged along behind it. I stuffed my Osprey hand in my coat pocket as that was the most recognizable thing about me.

Lost Property reception is on the main concourse. You can just see the acres of shadowy shelving through the door at the back. Happy to Help was there again. She wasn't Happy to Help.

'A leg?' she said. 'Weren't you here last week for a hand?'

'Yes.'

'And now you want a leg?'

'It's not for me. It's for a friend.'

'Can't your friend come and get their own leg?'

'No – because they've lost their leg. So they can't walk.'

'OK, I'll go and see. You don't mind waiting here?' She smiled.

It was not the smile of someone who smiles because they're happy. It was the smile of someone who has practised smiling in front of the mirror. For suspicious reasons. The smile of someone who wants you to stand there while she goes to tell security that that trouble-making kid is back.

I slipped away, pretending to be interested in the carnations in Up, Up and Bouquet until the coast was clear.

Then I ducked out of the airport and went to the Limb Lab.

Back at the airport, I'd had this idea that maybe I could secretly copy Eric's left leg, then hack into the 3D printer to make him a brand-new one. I took one look at the printer and realized I had no idea how to use it. Also, a leg made of resin and plastic was never going to hold up Eric's massive metal body.

Dr Shilling swept in. 'Right, team,' she said. 'It's time to Show Your Moves!'

Show Your Moves is when you have to demonstrate what progress you've made in learning to use your new limbs.

Tyler had progressed to playing the piano with his new fingers. There was no piano in the Limb Lab. His mum had brought one in specially – a little electric keyboard – just to show us. And he didn't play 'Happy Birthday' or 'Ten Green Bottles'. He played the theme from *Pirates of the Caribbean* – with drum effects – while his mum turned the pages of his music, looking very proud.

'How does his playing now compare to his playing before the accident?' asked Dr Shilling.

'He couldn't play at all before his accident,' said Tyler's mum.

'Couldn't play at all,' said Tyler, who seemed to think he needed to translate his mum as well as Shatter.

'Well, that *is* progress!' said Dr Shilling.

D'Arcy had taken up ballet. She pirouetted and performed *jeté*s all over the place on her blades. I know they're the right words, because she would keep saying them.

Shatter's karate looked more terrifying than ever.

And my progress was . . . no progress.

Not going to lie – I am impressed by the Osprey Grip MM. As hands go, it's one of the best. I love all its special grips: the key grip, for when I'm using keys or knives and forks; the power grip, for lifting things. It can do things no flesh-job hand could ever do – for instance, spin round completely on your wrist. Very useful for terrifying smaller people. I also love that I can synch it with my phone.

I just hadn't yet learned how to synch it with my brain.

Dr Shilling gave a little speech about the amazingness of my hand. 'Alfie will be able to operate it with his thoughts. Just imagine. In the very near future, engineers here in England could be sitting comfortably in their own homes, controlling hands like these to do all the heavy work millions of miles away, on Mars. Imagine a surgeon in London performing a delicate operation in Addis Ababa. And Alfie here is leading the way.'

She probably made this speech to motivate me. It didn't really work. It motivated Shatter, though, to fume and rage.

'Yeah, but,' she said, 'he can't! Work it.'

'He can't work his own hand,' said Tyler.

'He will in time,' said Dr Shilling. 'It's a question of motivation. When he finds something he really wants to do with his hand, he'll do it. Greatness doesn't come easy. Alfie is on a great quest for humanity. He's a pioneer.'

'Can't work his. Own fingers,' said Shatter.

Normally, by the time everyone has Shown Their Moves, I just want to go home and crawl into bed for a week. Not this time. I'd had another idea.

The Shilling Room is a kind of mini-museum of non-flesh limbs. It's named after Dr Shilling's grandad – the founder of the Limb Lab. I thought if I had a look in there I might find some kind of leg for Eric. They've got a whole history of wooden legs going back to pirate days. There's a display of artificial arms from the First World War hanging on the wall. When you open the door, the breeze makes them shiver like a skeletal Mexican wave.

I didn't notice Dr Shilling had come in behind me until she spoke.

'Amazing, isn't it, Alfie,' she said, 'how far we've come?'

'Amazing.'

'Were you looking for something in particular, Alfie?'

I could have said, 'Yes, I was looking for a spare

bionic leg for my secret robot.' But I thought it was probably wiser to say, 'Just looking. I wanted to know more about, you know, history and things.' So I did.

'That's really good. The more you know about history, the clearer you can see the future.' As if to prove it, she picked up a wooden leg and waggled it. 'This is the first ever false leg to have joints like a real leg. See? Made for the Marquess of Anglesey after he lost a leg at Waterloo in 1815. It's got both dorsiflexion and plantar flexion. Do you know what that means?'

'No.'

'Look it up. And, here – this is the first artificial hand Grandfather Shilling ever made.'

It looked like a big leather glove with some hinges and stuff inside.

'So you grew up in this house?' I asked.

'Well, in a flat inside the house. The house was full of offices and workshops when I was little. And children of course. They came here to learn how to use their new limbs. And not *just* to use them. Grandad thought the best people to help design new body parts were the people who were going to use them. So the children were taught how everything worked. Lots of them became inventors and engineers themselves. Some of the most exciting technology we use today was invented by Limb Lab kids. The Pizzabot? An ex-Limb Lab kid built that. And your

Osprey hand? Well, I designed that.'

'Thanks.'

'That's me when I was little in that photograph. And that's my father, Arthur Shilling, when he was little. It's always been a family firm. To help children who'd been injured in wars and accidents to have a better life. A quest, really. Like King Arthur. My grandparents loved anything to do with King Arthur. That's why they named my father Arthur.'

There were loads of photographs on the wall: some really old ones in black and white where the kids were wearing mad old-fashioned clothes; some more recent. In all the photographs, the kids were sitting at a big round table.

'Like in Camelot,' said Dr Shilling.

Not going to lie, I wasn't interested in the furniture. I just wanted to know if I could get Eric a spare leg here. I said, 'Did they ever invent any legs? I don't mean blades; I mean legs. Legs that can walk. Legs like on a walking robot?'

'Robots don't walk,' said Dr Shilling. 'I mean, some do, but they're not very good. Gimmicks mostly. We're not interested in things like that here at the Limb Lab. Asking a robot to walk is a waste of brainpower. Walking is an incredibly complicated and risky activity.'

I pointed out that the robots in *Stars Wars* can all

walk. 'They can walk and run and kick and everything.'

'They're not robots. They're actors in costumes. Take a look around the Limb Lab. Do we give people new legs? No – we give them blades. Think about it. What's the most precious thing in your body?' she said. 'The only bit you can't replace?'

'My brain?'

'Exactly. And where is your brain?' She picked up a little demonstration doll from the interactivity table. 'It's stuck in a little box on top of a wobbly neck, right at the top of your body where any enemy can take a swipe at it, and the whole thing is balanced on these two spindly fragile legs. Is that a good idea?'

'It's worked so far.'

'When you walk, watch what happens.' Dr Shilling made the little doll walk across the table. 'When you take a step forward, you are basically falling over. Then you save yourself just in time with your other leg. Then you fall over again with that leg. Then you save yourself again. Walking is basically just a series of narrowly avoided falls. Is that any way to carry around the human brain? No. It's rubbish.'

A voice behind me said, 'What about the mad. Robot that's on. The rampage? That's got. Legs.' Shatter had sloped into the Shilling Room with Tyler in tow.

Dr Shilling's eyes narrowed. 'As I understand it, the robot that has featured on the news lately does not have legs. It rides around on an automated trolley. And it has nothing whatsoever to do with us here at the Limb Lab.'

'I never said. It did,' said Shatter.

'If you know anything about the whereabouts of that robot, I want you to tell me.'

'You?' said Tyler. 'Not the police?'

'Me AND the police. That robot is bringing our work into disrepute. A robot is not an imitation human. It's a machine for doing a job. The only job that thing is doing is scaring people. And scared people are dangerous.'

Like I said, Eric is controversial.

'What about BB8?' said Shatter. 'BB8 is. Real. I know because he. Was in. A science. Museum.'

'BB8 doesn't have legs, Alfie,' said Tyler, as if I was the one who brought BB8 into the conversation.

'No. He doesn't,' snapped Dr Shilling. 'The fact is, people have tried making robots with legs in the past and it led to disaster. OK?'

It must have been obvious that we were both a bit surprised that she was so triggered by my question because she went all super nice after that.

'Maybe future humans,' she said, her face softening into a smile, 'will have wheels just like BB8. Then their brains will be safer. The future is wheels and blades, not legs. The future is children like you.'

The way she looked at me and Tyler and Shatter and D'Arcy, you could see that she thought we were a team. Friends.

I was buzzing like a phone on silent, thinking we could be the Kids of the Future, united in amazing technology, like Guardians of the Galaxy.

'The future is wheels,' announced Tyler.

'Yes!' I said. 'The future is wheels.'

'The future is. Me,' said Shatter. She leaped into the distance.

It was a shame there wasn't a bit more distance for Shatter to leap into, because when I got back to my workstation, she was sitting there waiting for me with a face that said we were not a team.

'Your arm,' she snarled, 'looks. Like Lego, Robot. Boy.'

'She called you Robot Boy,' explained Tyler.

'I heard,' I said.

But just in case I hadn't heard clearly, she said it again, going into a bit more detail this time. 'Robot. Boy. Your dad's. A robot your. Mum's a robot. Your little. Brother . . .'

I didn't wait for her to finish. Something about what she'd said triggered me. Before I'd even thought of anything to say, I'd turned round and shoved her. She went flying. When I say she went *flying*, she really did fly – right along the corridor, like a bowling ball scattering kids like skittles. The Osprey hand does pack a stronger-than-usual punch.

As she lay sprawled on the floor, I thought, *Oh great – more controversy.*

I got ready for her to come at me.

But she didn't. Shatter stood up, hands in the air. 'All right it's. All right,' she said.

Dr Shilling had come over by then. 'I see Alfie has made some progress after all,' she said. 'Though unarmed combat is not the kind of progress we were hoping for. Are you all right, Shatila?'

'I'm fine. It doesn't. Matter I. Just tripped.'

Maybe Shatter was making progress in kindness, I thought.

Wrong.

Before I even got to my workstation, she'd messaged me: Didn't. Batter you in. Class coz they'd've. Stopped me. Will kill. You soon.

It was interesting to me that she was just as stop-start when she was texting as when she was talking. Maybe she used voice recognition.

Tyler came over and said, 'Shatila is going to kill you. Sometime.'

I suppose he was worried that I hadn't got the text. 'I know.'

'She's annoyed that you pushed her.'

'I know.'

'Don't worry about it,' said D'Arcy. 'You've got a strong right fist. In this world, a strong right fist solves nearly every problem.'

You probably think I was scared. I wasn't.

I was just thinking, *The Future Is Wheels*.

STEP 11: KILLER ROBOT

Back home, I went straight to the shed to tell Eric my idea. He was surrounded by grow bags, big plant pots, a few collapsible chairs, a sun lounger, an old-fashioned electric kettle and some cushions. But, most of all, by memories. Memories seemed to rush out of that shed on the breeze. I couldn't tell you what they were memories *of* exactly. A feeling of remembering blew all around me, then seemed to vanish, like a song on the radio of a passing car. I felt I'd lost some big, shiny memory, just like I'd lost my hand.

Then I saw exactly what I was looking for, and I forgot all about my feelings. Sticking up from behind the pile of cardboard boxes – like a meerkat looking out for trouble – were the handles of my scooter. I'd forgotten I even had a scooter. As soon as I saw it, a memory was triggered – the scooter was something to do with my accident.

I went over to pick it up and, as I touched it, little flashes came back to me. As if the scooter was a USB stick, and I'd stored bits of memory in it.

I let the memory go.

I was far too busy to think about stuff like that now.

I hoisted the scooter out from behind the boxes. Apparently it had come out of the accident without a scratch. Mum must have put it in the shed until I was ready to ride it again. It's got a telescopic steering column, so you can make it as tall or as small as you like.

You can, for instance, make it exactly the same size as Eric's leg. Which is what I did.

'Eric,' I said, 'what if you had a scooter for a leg? One leg could be the scooter, and the other leg could scoot. I'll show you.'

I stepped on to the scooter to show him how it worked.

I AM YOUR OBEDIENT SERVANT.

'Good. Follow me.'

Out in the yard, I wedged the handlebars into the slot at the bottom of his torso where his left leg went, turned it round until it I couldn't any more, and tightened all the screws. The running board was also extendable. I jiggled it round until it was the same size as Eric's foot. It had two wee whizz wheels, one on each end.

'Right, Eric. Give it a whirl.'

Eric tried a step. The scooter shot forward from under him. He should have fallen backwards, but his other leg came down just in time to stop him. He tried it again.

And again.

And again.

IF YOU WILL PERMIT ME . . .

'Yeah, go ahead. Keep practising.'

It was working! The sun slithered over Eric's metal panels as he moved. He was upright and mobile. When he wobbled into the gate, it swung open.

'Eric, don't go out.'

I AM YOUR OBEDIENT SERVANT, said Eric, going out.

'Do you actually even know what *obedient* means?'

I'M SORRY. I CAN'T ANSWER THAT QUESTION.

He rumbled over the concrete patio of the yard. He wobbled through the gate. He scooted – proper scooted – down the alley.

'Eric! Don't go far!'

At the very end of the alley, he spun round and scooted back towards me; then he stopped and spun round again. He spread his arms out and aeroplaned back down the alley. His steel fingers struck sparks all along the backyard walls.

The sparks made other memories flash in my head – I remembered plunging down underpasses on my scooter on bright sunny days. Scooting along walkways.

I KNOW HUNDREDS OF JOKES.

He whooped, in a way that seemed to say, 'I'm really chuffing chuffed with myself.' He shot to the far end of the alley, turned left, and then . . .

He disappeared.

'No! Eric! Come back!'

I tore after him. Out of the alley, on to Stealth Street. When I caught up with him, he was holding on to a lamp post with one hand, spinning himself round it. For a machine that had no emotions, he was doing a brilliant job of looking really happy. He sounded like a hundred dustbins having a party.

'Eric, slow down! You're going to fall!'

I AM YOUR OBEDIENT SERVANT.

Then he clattered on to the pavement.

'Eric?' I cried. 'What's happening? Are you dead?'

No. Eric's a machine. Not a person. He'd never been alive, so he couldn't be dead. Machines are not like people. If a machine stops working, you can fix it. Like I said, with machines, there is always a way to fix them. You just need to stay calm and think.

What I thought was . . . batteries. What if Eric just needed recharging?

I searched his body for some kind of socket. There were three metal spikes sticking out of his neck like the prongs that stick out of the bottom of an old-fashioned kettle when you pull the electric cord out. I knew because I'd just seen a kettle like that in the shed.

I dashed back to the shed, grabbed the kettle lead, and returned quickly to Eric. It slotted snugly over his spikes.

Great! All I had to do was plug him into one of the DustUrchin recharging points. There was one on every lamp post.

Except the lead was only about half a metre long.

And the nearest lamp post was on the other side of the road. How was I going to move half a ton of steel across the road? Easy! Extension lead. Great. There was one in the shed. I ran and got it. Plugged him in. All I needed now was for the road to stay completely deserted for the next . . . how long?

How long was it going to take? It takes about half an hour to charge my phone, and Eric is about a million times bigger. What if it took half a million hours? I was panicking that, any minute now, the empty pavements would be full of kids coming home from school, and everyone would know about Eric.

I crouched over his body, willing him to recharge more quickly. I was thinking that even if he just got to three per cent I could probably move him back to the shed before anyone saw him.

All the time Eric was lying alone on the pavement, my heart was in my mouth. Luckily there was no one around. Everyone was at school or at work.

After a few minutes, there was a faint tinkling. Well, not *tinkling* exactly; more of a rattle with a squeak thrown in. The sort of noise you hear if there's a coin rolling around in the glove compartment of your car. Then Eric's eyes started to glow slightly. Eric was charging up.

Then I heard a faint whirring sound overhead. The lamp post's CCTV camera was focusing in on us. If you're going to keep a secret on the Skyways Estate, you have to hide it from lamp posts as well as people.

Then people turned up.

A driverless bus stopped just across the road, and people got out. Lots of people. Kids. In uniform. The uniform of Skyways High ('Aiming Higher'). My school.

Someone spotted me. 'Look! It's Alfie Miles!'

They all flocked across the road towards me. As they got closer, names popped into my head one after the other, like something was being uploaded into my brain.

Dr Shilling had given us special lessons on how to cope when your old friends meet your new limb.

'Some of them will be freaked out,' she'd said. 'They might be rude or cruel. Mostly that just means they're scared or uncomfortable. Which means you're in control. It's up to you to put them at ease. Tell them a joke. For instance, say, "Do you need a hand?" Then take your hand off and offer it to them. Works every time. Ha ha.'

Freaking people out seemed like the best tactic for me at that moment. At least it distracted them from the massive illegal robot on the pavement.

As they got nearer, I could hear them talking.

'I thought Alfie Miles was killed in a tragic accident?'

'Not killed, just hideously mangled.'

I lifted my Osprey hand. For one second, it was like I'd pressed the mute button on life. Everyone stared.

125

The next second, it was noisier than ever. They were yelling and squashing and clambering over each other to try to get a better view.

'Is that yours?'

'Is that real?'

'Does it come off?'

Literally no one was looking at Eric. Only at me. In fact, some people were standing on him so that they could see me better.

When everyone is staring at you, you've got options.

You can run and hide.

You can curl up like a hedgehog.

Or you can give them something to stare at.

So, I wrenched my own hand off, and I held it out for them to see. First, they screamed and backed off. Then they gasped and leaned forward.

'Can I hold it?'

That was a girl I used to sit next to in Padre Pio Primary. She had the reddest hair on the planet, but I couldn't remember her name. And she couldn't wait for a reply. She just grabbed my hand and held it away from her like she was holding a tarantula. She prodded it with her fingernail.

'Can you feel that?'

'No. Of course not. It's not even connected to my arm.'

'If I bend the finger back, will it hurt?' She bent

the middle finger backwards until the tip touched the wrist. 'Ohmygoditgoesrightback! What's his name? Has he got a name?'

It was really rattling me now that I couldn't remember this girl's name, so I said, 'Tell him your name, and maybe he'll tell you his.'

'You mean he can talk? Like if you talk to the hand, the hand talks back! That's so amusing. And it's a he. Is it a he?'

'Well, I'm a boy, so, yeah, I'm going to have boy hands.'

'Hello, Hand. My name's Maria-Jaoa. What's yours?'

Maria-Jaoa! Now I remembered. She was always saying, 'Ohmygodsocute!' about various people and things.

I said, 'He doesn't have a name. Why should he have a name? Does your hand have a name?'

When she let go of it, the hand opened up like a flower.

'Ohmygodsocute! I'm going to call him Lefty.'

I did try pointing out that it was my *right* hand, but she said that was the joke. I could have tried pointing out that it really wasn't down to her to think of names for parts of me, but it was already too late. Everyone loved the name Lefty.

At the Limb Lab, they told us that giving a name

to your new state-of-the-art limb made it easier for people to relate to it. But they never explained that it would be THIS easy. Within about ten seconds of being given the name, Lefty had a crowd of admirers. If you check now, you'll see he's got his own Facebook group: 'Friends of Lefty'. If I call into Skyways High now, more people know Lefty's name than know mine. I'm not Alfie Miles there; I'm just Lefty's human appendage.

Not going to lie – I actually was having a good time at that point. I forgot that Eric was in danger. I gave a kind of demonstration on How Lefty Works. I showed them how you could press the fingers back into the hand or lock them into different positions: hanger, shovel, fist, palm, pointer.

I didn't say, 'The hand doesn't really need me to move its fingers. It could do all these things with a thought. If I could just think the right thought.'

Instead I said, 'So who wants to shake hands with Lefty?'

Oh, they loved that. They formed a queue.

Most of them weren't satisfied with just a handshake. Most people wanted a selfie.

When I got bored, I pulled the middle finger clean off. A beam of light shot out from the inbuilt torch, and I said, 'Sorry, sorry – that's the laser! Better get back, everyone!'

And everyone backed off, laughing.

Then, behind my back, Eric began to shake. He was almost recharged. He was trying to stand up. I had to get rid of them.

Easy.

I put my hand down on the floor and said, 'Everyone! Watch Lefty!' So even I was calling my hand Lefty now.

I ran up to the corner of Stealth Street and turned my phone on. I couldn't actually see Lefty from there, but I could hear the pretend screams and laughs as he began to spider crawl along the pavement towards me.

They followed him all the way to me. They all said it was the coolest thing ever and asked me when I was going to come back to school.

'Soon,' I said.

'We weren't talking to you,' said one of the girls. 'We were talking to Lefty!'

Everyone laughed and went home.

Maria–Jaoa lived on Spitfire Street so she walked back with me, which was awkward. Because we had to pass Eric.

'Oh my God,' she said. 'It's that killer robot. The one that's been rampaging around killing kids.' She was one of those people who thought the news always understated things so you had to exaggerate to get the truth.

'Oh no,' I assured her. 'That's not a robot. That's a project.'

'What kind of project?'

'From the Limb Lab school. We have to make stuff, so I'm making a suit of armour.'

'It's got a scooter instead of a leg.'

I said, 'Yeah. So?' and looked meaningfully at Lefty.

'Oh.' Maria-Jaoa blushed. 'I get it. It's a suit of armour for someone with no leg. Awkward. Sorry. I bet loads of knights only had one leg. I bet the best ones only had one leg because they lost the other one in battle.'

'Exactly,' I said. 'Well, see you soon.'

'See you, Alfie. See you, Lefty.'

I let Lefty wave to her.

A few minutes later, Eric was upright so I unplugged him, and we scooted back home. As soon as we were back in the shed, he said:

WATER LEVEL IS LOW.

'You need water?'

He opened his mouth really wide and tipped his head back.

I rushed into the house, got a jug of water and poured it down his throat. Then I started to worry. Surely water and electricity are a fatal combination? Steam began to come out of Eric's ears. There was a banging in his chest. I backed away to the shed door, ready to dive for cover if he exploded. Then a panel in his chest popped open. He reached inside and pulled out . . . a camping kettle.

FOUR O'CLOCK, he said. **TIME FOR TEA.**

He held the kettle on his open hand, and his palm began to heat up. Soon the kettle was singing like a bird. With his other hand, he pulled out of his chest a china teapot decorated with flowers, two china cups and saucers, and a milk jug.

LEAVE TO BREW FOR FIVE MINUTES.

Obviously there was no tea in the pot and no milk in the jug.

SHALL I BE MOTHER?

He poured some hot water into the tea cups. I sipped it politely and chatted to him about the day. He kept nodding his head. Maybe making tea was his way of saying thanks for fixing his leg.

Not going to lie, when I decided to fix up a massive illegal robot, I thought I might need to find lasers or weaponry for him. Instead, I ended up promising to get him some fresh milk and tea and sugar from the Co-op.

When Mum came home that night, she rushed right at me, saying, 'Are you all right? Are you all right?'

'Yeah. Why?'

'I heard that a bunch of Skyways High kids had you surrounded at the bus stop. Were they bullying you?'

'No.'

'Are you sure?'

'To be honest,' I said, 'I sort of gave them the impression that my new hand had laser capabilities.'

She laughed, and I said, 'Nice cup of tea?'

She said, 'Ta.'

A few minutes later, Mum was in the kitchen, wondering why her tea wasn't ready. 'I only wanted a mug of tea, Alfie – a mug with a tea bag and some hot water in it. Not a dress rehearsal for the queen's garden party.'

I looked down at the tray. It's true; we usually made tea in a mug with a tea bag. Maybe hanging out with Eric had made me a bit more – I don't know – formal. I'd made tea in the teapot and put it on a tray with proper cups and saucers, napkins, a china sugar bowl and milk in a jug. The sugar bowl was probably a bit much, especially as neither of us take sugar.

'Sorry. It's ready now.'

'I'm only teasing. I think it's lovely.'

'You know,' I said, 'the kids from school were really nice. They even gave my hand a name. Lefty.'

'But it's a right hand.'

'I know. That's the joke.'

'Oh, I see.' She laughed again. 'Maybe that will

help. Giving it a name. If you think of your hand as a pet rather than a hand, maybe that will help give it some, you know, life. Like I do with Ollie.'

Ollie is what she calls the DustUrchin. Ollie the Omnivore. To demonstrate, she dropped a pinch of sugar on the lino and said, 'Come on, Ollie. Come on, little fella . . .'

The Dust Urchin came scuttling over and sucked up the sugar.

'See? The more you talk to a thing, the more alive it gets. You have to put some of yourself in there.'

'The kids in school,' I said, 'were actually nicer than the kids in the Limb Lab. Maybe I should go back to school instead of the Limb Lab.'

'Definitely,' said Mum. 'The moment you bring Lefty to life. The day you make his fingers move, you can go back to school and all your old friends. That's what we agreed.'

'Right.'

'All you need is a little imagination.'

STEP 12: HUMAN VERSUS ROBOT

Next morning, when I got to Limb Lab, Tyler and D'Arcy were waiting for me.

'Shatila is going to beat you up,' said Tyler.

'I know.'

'She's annoyed that you pushed her.'

'I know.'

In fact, the whole of Limb Lab seemed to know. When I was walking over to my workstation, people kept patting me on the back, wishing me luck and saying things like, 'It was nice knowing you.'

Shatter kept away from me all day. I started to hope that she'd forgotten all about it. Maybe she'd moved on to some other fight. But at home time there she was – waiting at the gates.

I took my coat off as I strode towards her. I was hoping that if I made it obvious there was going to be a scrap a grown-up would interfere. I even gave Shatter a little shove when I got to her. She put her hands up.

'If I get. Into a. Fight on Limb Lab property,' she said, 'I get. Excluded.'

Apparently she'd been excluded from ten schools before she even came to Limb Lab.

'I've made other. Arrangements,' she said, 'for the. Fight.'

D'Arcy wheeled Shatter's bike towards Concorde Circus. There was a bit of plastic she had taped to the mudguard, which clicked against the spokes as the wheel turned. *Tick tick tick*, like a bomb waiting to go off.

Shatter tried to spark up a conversation. 'Best place for. A fight,' she explained. 'Under the. Tree. We can really batter. Each. Other. It's in the. Middle of a traffic. Island, so if any. One tries to stop. Us they'll have to. Wait for traffic to. Clear before they. Can get to us. So we'll have. Time to. Scatter. Plus. Loads of people can come and. Watch us. There's no point having a. Massive fight if no one. Is watching.'

'So this is going to be a massive fight?'

'It's me versus you. Human versus.

Robot. Alien. Versus Predator. There is a LOT of. Interest in this fight.'

We were on the traffic island by this point. I looked over my shoulder. Remember the bit in *The Lion King* where all the wildebeest come pouring over the hill? That's how many people were crossing the road to watch this fight. Kids from the Limb Lab. Kids from Skyways High (Aiming Higher). Kids I'd never seen in my life. There were going to be a lot of witnesses to my final destruction.

I held my hand up. 'Just need a bit of a warm-up.'

'Don't be. Long,' said Shatter. 'I've got. Ballet.'

'You do *ballet*?'

'Why shouldn't I. Do ballet?'

'No reason.'

I clamped Lefty's fingers together, folded them over, clambered up and hooked them over the lowest branch of the tree. I grabbed on with my other hand and started doing chin-ups.

'Good idea,' said Shatter. 'I'll do. The same.'

Except it wasn't the same. When Shatter did chin-ups, all her weight was going to her muscles. When I did chin-ups, all my weight was going to Lefty's steel and resin joints. Steel and resin don't get tired. Muscles do.

After ten chin-ups, Shatter was looking a bit sweaty.

After fifteen, she was starting to wince a bit with the pain.

Lefty didn't sweat. Lefty didn't feel pain. I carried on chinning up.

By the time I got to twenty, I knew I could do this all night.

By the time SHE got to twenty, Shatter was losing her grip.

Maria-Jaoa was in the crowd. She started chanting 'Lef-ty! Lef-ty! Lef-ty!'

Other people joined in. 'Lef-ty! Lef-ty! Lef-ty!'

Shatter grunted. Her legs were flailing.

I decided to speed things up. If I could turn this whole thing into a chin-ups contest instead of a fight, I'd dodge the battering.

If Shatter has one world-class skill, however, it is making sure that people do not dodge a battering. She dropped from the branch like an angry ripe apple. She put her hands on her hips and said, 'I'm warmed. Up. You're warmed. Up. Let's. Fight, Robot Boy.'

I was expecting the crowd to cheer. Or boo. Or grunt.

But nothing.

They just stood there, mouths open, eyes staring.

Not staring at me.

Not staring at Shatter.

Staring at something behind us.

I didn't have to turn round to see what it was. I could hear the grinding gears, the creaking metal.

WE WANT A GOOD, CLEAN FIGHT . . .

'What is. THAT?' Shatter was scrambling backwards.

'She wants to know what that is,' said Tyler, staring at Eric, his eyes bulging out of his head.

I AM ERIC, THE WORLD'S MOST POLITE ROBOT. HOW DO YOU DO, AND WHO ARE YOU?

Steam came out of Eric's nostrils, and a terrible gurgling started up in his throat. I glanced at my phone. Four o'clock. Eric had come to find me for tea.

I understand that if you don't know that Eric is only making tea, then Eric's tea-making style – steam billowing from his nose, his insides gurgling hungrily – can look a bit intimidating.

Shatter almost knocked me over trying to run away.

NO PUSHING, SHOVING OR WRESTLING! boomed Eric.

'I wasn't. Pushing, shoving or. Wrestling!' protested Shatter. 'I was trying to run away.'

'She's trying to run away,' explained Tyler, running away.

WE WANT A GOOD, CLEAN FIGHT, ACCORDING TO THE RULES LAID DOWN BY THE MARQUESS OF QUEENSBERRY IN 1867.

'Actually, I don't want a good, clean fight,' said D'Arcy. 'I want to get out of here.'

NO KICKING OR BITING. EACH BOUT WILL LAST THREE MINUTES. NO SHOES ARE TO BE WORN. KINDLY REMOVE YOUR SHOES . . .

'I'm not taking my shoes off. I'm going home.'

IF ONE CONTESTANT IS KNOCKED DOWN, THAT CONTESTANT MUST GET UP AGAIN WITHIN TEN SECONDS OR BE CONSIDERED KNOCKED OUT. NOW, GENTLEMEN, FISTS UP.

Shatter pointed out that she wasn't a gentleman. Eric didn't seem to mind. His voice was so loud and so certain that you just had to do what he said. We both put our fists up like boxers in an old painting.

WE WILL ALL NOW STAND FOR THE NATIONAL ANTHEM. GOD SAVE OUR GRACIOUS KING . . . !

People covered their ears. Leaves fell from the tree, blown off by the sheer racket.

CONTESTANTS MUST STAY IN THEIR CORNERS UNTIL THE BELL.

From somewhere deep inside Eric's head, a bell rang – louder than any bell you've ever heard. Shatter tried to dodge around the roots of the tree, but Eric reached down and hoisted her into the air. She squirmed. She yelped.

Normally, when you pass Shatter in the Limb Lab corridor, she looks like a tractor in a hoodie. Now, dangling from Eric's mighty hand, she looked more like a little worried kitten.

'Let me. Go!' she screeched.

'Oh. Don't say *that*!' I warned. 'Eric takes things quite literally.'

'She wants you to let go!' said Tyler.

I AM YOUR OBEDIENT SERVANT.

He let go.

Shatter fell.

She pancaked into the crowd. She jumped to her feet, snarling and staring. 'Oh. My. God,' she steamed. 'His dad really is a robot.'

And then it was *Lion King* wildebeest time again. Every kid stampeded off over the road and out of sight.

I said, 'Thanks, Eric.'

THE WINNER!

He took my hand and held it up above my head in a victory salute. Except there was no one to salute. There were no kids left in sight.

The 81A bus was tootling towards us up Hurricane Way. 'Eric,' I said, 'let's go home. We can catch the bus.'

STEP 13: I ORDERED PEPPERONI PIZZA!

Eric takes things literally. Which is why – about two seconds after I said, 'Eric, let's catch the bus' – there was a squeal of brakes.

At first, I couldn't even look. The sound of those brakes set other sounds rushing out of my memory: the sound of a scooter clattering over; a terrible splodge that might have been my old hand slapping to the ground.

The sounds of The Accident.

Then someone shouted, and I opened my eyes.

The bus was in the middle of the road. Eric had grabbed hold of its bumper. He'd stopped it with his bare hands. Now he was crouching down with his head back as if he was trying to lift the bus up.

'Eric, what are you doing?'

YOU ASKED ME TO CATCH THE BUS. IT TRIED TO ESCAPE BUT I CAUGHT IT. I AM YOUR OBEDIENT SERVANT.

He yanked on the bus. I *swear* it jerked forward.

The next one to speak was the bus. The words came

from deep inside its cab. '*I am a scheduled, driverless service,*' it said. '*In the interests of passenger safety and schedules, please remove the obstruction.*'

The bus spoke again, but this time its words came out quite hiccoughy because Eric was shaking the whole bus up and down and yanking it from side to side.

'*For safety safety reasons reasons,*' it stuttered, '*all passengers please please please leave leave the bus. Please leave the bus until the bus is returned to the ground.*'

Luckily there were no passengers inside it, but people were coming out of the Co-op to see what the noise was about. The woman from the meat counter strode over, her meat cleaver sticking out of the pocket of her white overalls.

'It's that robot off the news!' she growled.

'No! No!' It was a girl's voice that said this. Maria-Jaoa had come trotting after her, clutching a fistful of chocolate bars. 'It's a suit of armour – isn't it, Alfie?'

'Yeah, a suit of armour,' I said. 'School project. We've got to go.'

'It's only got one leg,' said the woman with the meat cleaver.

'SO what!' snarled Maria-Jaoa. 'Don't you think there were one-legged knights in days of old? They were in wars, you know. There's nothing wrong with

144

only having one leg. Or one hand. Or whatever. Is there, Alfie?'

'Errrm. That's right. Let's go, Eric.'

The meat-cleaver woman was still giving us the hard stare.

'Eric is my friend's name,' I said. 'He's inside the armour. Like a knight.'

The word 'knight' seemed to trip some kind of switch in Eric's memory. He stood very tall. His head swivelled round to look down on the cleaver woman. His eyes flashed – literally, of course. He said:

VARLET!

Varlet is an insult used in days of yore by knights of old. I did not take it as a good sign that Eric was being rude, even in an antique way.

'Got to go,' I said.

WE RIDE AT DAWN!

'Exactly,' I said. 'So we're already late. Hurry up.'

I walked off, trusting that he'd follow me, which he did. As far as the corner of Typhoon Street.

A Pizzabot was coming the other way.

Eric stopped right in front of it.

The Pizzabot said, '*Scusi, per piacere.*'

STAND ASIDE, VARLET!

'*Pizza for thirty-two Typhoon Street, scusi. He's a-gonna go cold.*'

ASIDE, VARLET!

'*Scusi. Pizza for thirty-two Typhoon . . .*'

ASIDE . . .

'*He's a-gonna go cold.*'

It seemed like Eric would be happy to spend the entire day arguing with an oven. I told him to let the Pizzabot get on with his job.

I STAND ASIDE FOR NO MAN.

'It's not a man, though, is it? It's an oven. On wheels.'

NOR YET FOR ANY UNNATURAL FIEND.

There really did seem to be a lot of knight-related words hidden in his memory.

'Seriously, it's an oven. Walk away. If you're a knight, then surely you've got a quest to be getting on with.'

A KNIGHT DOES NOT RUN FROM HIS FOE.

Different people have different ideas about how to make the world a better place. You might want to clean up the oceans or stop global warming. Knights of old wanted to kill dragons or find the Holy Grail. It seemed Eric had decided to make the world a better place by fighting a pizza oven.

'*I've tried asking nicely,*' said the Pizzabot. '*Now get outta the way.*'

AN INSULT! WITHDRAW OR FIGHT LIKE A GENTLEMAN.

'It's not a gentleman, Eric,' I said. 'It's a Pizzabot. According to Descartes – who is the main person when it comes to robots – it's got no free will. How can you insult someone if they've got no free will?'

WITHDRAW THE INSULT OR SUFFER THE CONSEQUENCES.

Eric reached over and grabbed a garlic baguette from the oven's side pocket. He held it like a sword, stretching one arm behind his back.

The oven tried to barge past him.

GENTLEMEN DO NOT BRAWL.. THEY DUEL. FIRST, SALUTE.

He raised the baguette to his face in a kind of greeting, then pointed it menacingly at the oven's middle.

I was feeling sorry for the oven by now. It tried to sidle past him again. Eric whacked it with the garlic bread, and when that broke into a thousand crumbs he crushed the hot little Pizzabot so hard between his mighty hands that the pizza popped out of the top and frisbee'd into my hands.

'Now look what you've done!' I bawled, struggling to balance the pizza. 'What am I supposed to do with this?'

It was the first time I'd ever shouted at Eric.

Eric's reaction to being shouted at? He tried to tell his fish joke again.

WHAT KIND OF FISH DOES A SEA MONSTER EAT? NO, THAT JOKE IS INCORRECT.

Robots can't cry. I think getting a fish joke wrong is maybe the robot way of saying, 'I'm sad.' Eric's arms hung down at his side, and the blue light of his eyes dimmed.

'Come on,' I said. 'You can carry the pizza. Let's go and deliver it. It's the least we could do.'

I pressed the doorbell of number 32. Eric probably thought that if he copied what I did, he would be sure to be doing the right thing. So he pressed the doorbell too. When I touched the doorbell, it chimed. When Eric touched the doorbell, it clanged like a fire alarm. Every light in the house started flashing on and off. Radios and TVs blasted out at full volume. Smoke alarms howled. Eric's finger seemed to be activating every electrical appliance in the building.

A teenage boy in a big T-shirt, big earphones and an even bigger state of panic pulled the door open, his eyes bulging with fear.

'What? What's going on?' he said, looking up and down the street as if there might be an invasion.

'Pizza!' I said, as though that explained everything.

And Eric hurled the pizza through the open door. It flew along the hallway and landed perfectly on the kitchen table.

'Enjoy,' I said. 'Good shot, by the way, Eric.'

THANK YOU.

'Hey!' yelled the boy as I steered Eric away. 'I ordered pepperoni! This is tuna!'

Once we were back on the street, I said, 'Eric, you're supposed to be lying low . . .'

His knees began to bend. I knew what was coming. He was going to lie low – literally.

I yelled, 'NO! Don't lie down. Not here. You're an outlaw. You're not supposed to draw attention to yourself.'

GOOD SHOT.

'Yes, it was a good shot,' I reassured him. 'Now let's go home.'

There was a high whining sound coming from somewhere overhead.

A delivery drone was hovering over the rooftops, its spindly body wobbling in the air like a skeleton bird of prey. Delivery drones hover for a bit, make sure that no one is in the way, then they swoop down and leave a parcel on your doorstep. Normally.

That's not what happened today. The drone swept over the roofs, but it didn't deliver anything. It swung up and down the street, and each time it passed by, it came nearer.

'Eric,' I said, 'I think we're being watched.'

GOD SAVE OUR . . .

'No. Don't do that. Let's get out of here as quick as we can.'

I've got to admit, he was obedient. When I said that about being quick, he plonked me on his shoulders and hurtled off along the avenue. When I say *hurtled*, I mean that every rivet in his body was shaking. But the drone came after us, its whine getting higher and higher. We dived into an underpass, scooter wheels thundering. The drone was waiting for us when we shot out of the other side.

Eric paused and looked up. The drone hovered closer. Eric's eyes blazed blue. Then he swatted the drone out of the sky like a fly. It tumbled on to the tarmac. The lens of its camera twinkled in the dust.

'Oh!' I gasped. 'You should not have done that. You definitely should not have done that.'

Eric just spread his giant arms wide and aeroplaned off around the traffic island. Sparks flew from his wheels where he clipped the paving stones.

'Eric!' I yelled. 'Where are we going?'

I AM YOUR OBEDIENT SERVANT, he said.

He curved across the car park of the Community Hub. He sailed past the DustHog enclosure. There's a low wooden fence behind it. He smashed through that, and then we were thundering through Hangar Wood.

STEP 14: HANGAR WOOD

The only bad thing about the Skyways estate is the possibility that something will fall out of the sky and crush you, or destroy your house. For instance, two brothers from my old school, Christian and Benedict Walker, went out to feed their rabbits one day, and there was this thing sitting there in the yard. A gold cube. The rabbit hutch was in splinters. All the rabbits were in a circle staring at this big shiny gold cube. They were all like, what could that even be? A bit that's fallen off the sun? Or off the Transformers' AllSpark?

They went and got their mum, and by the time they got back in the yard, this thing had started to melt. And it wasn't a piece of the sun, and it was nothing to do with Transformers. You could tell what it was from the smell.

It was a massive block of frozen pee. A huge Pee Popsicle that had fallen out of a plane. It purely stank. All his rabbits were twitching their noses. One of them – Billy Bob Bobtail – had literally passed out from the stench.

Anyway, their mum messaged the airport and, the next thing they knew, some cleaning people turned up In special uniform!

So that's how often things fall out of the sky around here. There is a dedicated Pee Popsicle Disposal Unit with its own uniform.

Then there's the Legend of the Haunted Hangar. Back in the day, there used to be a factory near the airport that made aeroplanes. When it closed down, they turned the site into Hangar Wood. It's called Hangar Wood because the old hangars are still in there. In the spring, everyone goes there to see the carpet of dazzling bluebells. The rest of the year, people go there so their dogs can poo.

The story is that one night, years and years back, something fell out of the sky through one of the hangar roofs. Some people say it didn't even fall off a plane; it just fell out of the sky, like a meteor. The Thing was . . . Well, no one knows what it was. But you can still see the hole.

That's where Eric was heading. The Haunted Hangar.

He went straight there. Like he was looking for something.

He scooted along the marked paths. When they forked, he always seemed to know which way he was going to turn. When they were overgrown, he smashed through the brambles. When it got muddy, he kicked his way through, until we were standing in front of the ruined hangar.

The main building was hunched in the undergrowth like a big sleepy beast. Attached to its front – like a head – was something that looked like a little ruined house. It must have been the office one time, or the reception area. The slates were gone from its roof. Its windows were shattered. It was definitely empty. So how come when we walked past it, it made a noise?

It was probably just the wind rattling the windows, but it sounded like the house had coughed to get my attention.

The sound came again. It was a sound I'd heard somewhere before – a kind of metal slap – but I couldn't remember where.

If I hadn't had a massive robot bodyguard with me, I would have fled the scene. But Eric kept going.

He barged past the house and stopped in front of the hangar itself. Its curved walls were crusted with brambles and ivy and woodbine, like an ancient ruined castle in a fairy story. Eric grabbed a fistful of thorns and yanked them aside. There was an old half-rotten wooden door hanging off its rusted hinges. Through the gaps at the side, you could see into the huge cavern of the hangar.

'That building,' I said, 'is unsafe, and possibly haunted by some alien thing.'

Eric turned his head towards me.

'Which means,' I went on, 'it's exactly the hiding place we're looking for. Well done, Eric. Only problem is, I'm too scared to go inside.'

Eric pulled the door off its hinges as easily as you might pull blackberries off brambles. There was a pitter of falling rust. He stepped inside.

I was about to tread where no one had dared to tread in years.

This is it, I thought. *I am actually going to see the Thing-That-Fell-Out-of-the-Sky.*

What if it's something terrible?

What if it was something alive?

What if it was something dead?

I snapped back Lefty's middle finger and opened up its hi-beam torch. The hangar was so vast that the torchlight did not even reach the ceiling. It just melted

156

in a mist of dust and cobwebs. On the floor, a mess of broken wood and paint pots sent their shadows racing round the walls. Directly above the mess was a jagged gap in the roof. The legendary hole in the roof of the hangar. The very spot where the Thing had crashed through back in the day. The mess on the floor must be from where it crash-landed.

'Well,' I said, trying to sound un-scared, 'whatever fell through the roof definitely hit the floor hard. And whatever it was has gone now. So that's good.'

That's what I said. But what I was thinking was, *What if that's what's hiding in the little house?*

Shadows swept past me like ghosts. I swung round. Eric's eyes were blazing brighter than ever. His head was swinging from side to side, and up and down, like when your dog is trying to follow a smell.

I'd never seen him act like this before. I said, 'What's going on Eric? Are you looking for something? You came straight here as soon as we stepped into the woods. Did you know this place was here?'

I AM LOST.

His voice echoed around like a sad bell.

Just then, a plane thundered past low overhead. Its flashing tail lights lit up the hangar.

Not going to lie – I ducked. It was so low and loud.

Eric looked up at it and said:

I AM LOST.

'Come on, Eric. Let's go.'

WHY DO MONSTERS EAT SHIPS?

'Telling jokes isn't going to help.'

THE JOKE IS INCORRECT.

'Even if it was a really funny joke, I'd still want to go home. Before it gets dark.'

I AM LOST.

He sounded like he really didn't want to be left on his own.

'I wish I knew how to turn you off or put you into sleep mode, or something. Then you wouldn't mind—'

ACTIVATING BATTERY-SAVING MODE.

His head drooped. He sank to the floor with his leg and his scooter stretched out in front of him. The lights in his eyes and mouth went out.

Well, I thought, *that was easy enough*. I found an old tarpaulin and covered him up so that even if anyone did come after him they wouldn't see him. Then I left.

It was so good to be back in the fresh air I forgot to worry about the little house, until I was passing it and I heard that slap of metal again.

This time, I recognized it.

I don't know how I didn't recognize it before. After all, my mum is a postwoman. It was the sound of a letterbox flapping shut.

At the Limb Lab, they give us lessons about how to deal with fear.

'If you're scared of something,' says Dr Shilling, 'turn round and face it. Imagination magnifies fear Turn round, and you may see that you are being chased by a puppy, not a tiger.'

This advice turned out to be dead wrong.

I know because I did turn around. I did walk over to the door. I faced the Letterbox of Fear. I walked right up to it.

I crouched, lifted open the flap, and looked inside.

There was an eye.

A human eye.

Looking back at me.

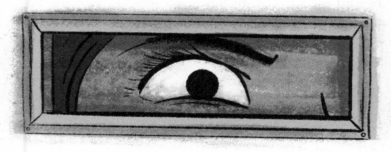

BANG!

I let the flap fall.

I ran all the way home.

STEP 15: ROGUE ROBOT

My heart was still going like the clappers when I got home. Even the front door noticed it. *'Come in, Alfie. Your heartbeat is significantly raised. Have you been running? I'll put the kettle on. Why not sit down and stabilize your metabolism?'*

Mum wasn't home. Normally I don't mind that much. After all, the house always says hello, and the DustUrchin tells me the news. And for the last few days Eric had filled the house with tension and thrills.

But now I really just wanted a human to talk to. Where was Mum? I hadn't even noticed until then, but she seemed to be home less than ever since my accident.

I opened one of the kitchen cupboards. It said, *'Hi Alfie! I've got tins of beans, tins of tuna. There's bread in the bread bin and cheese in the fridge. Serving suggestion: Why not make a delicious tuna melt? If you need recipe help, ask the cooker.'*

I wasn't going to be bossed around by a cupboard, so I went for beans on toast.

One good thing is I can use Lefty's inbuilt can opener to open the tin. I just put my finger on the top, it latches on to the tin, spins it round and there you go – it's open. It felt so cool I could have opened every tin in the house just for the fun of it. But what was the point when there was no one there to see it.

When I sat down to eat, the TV announced it had picked a news item that might interest me. '*Your teacher is on TV. Shall I stream it for you, Alfie?*'

'Yes, please.'

There was a whole thing about Eric on the news. It showed the CCTV footage that the drone had shot of him crashing around the estate with me on his shoulders. It ended with a blurry whirl, where Eric had whacked the drone out of the sky.

'*Robots,*' said the reporter '*are an essential part of all our lives. We live alongside them. They do the jobs we don't want to do. But what happens when robots go rogue? We ask someone who knows the answer better than anyone. Police Officer Grady.*'

Police Officer Grady turned out to be the very police officer whose car Eric had crushed. The answer to the question, 'What happens when robots go rogue?' seemed to be, 'It makes Police Officer Grady sad.' Because, not going to lie, he looked like he'd been crying for a week.

Officer Grady: '*This is one bad robot. He's assaulted a*

162

Pizzabot, wrecked a drone and gleefully and maliciously destroyed my car.'

Reporter: 'That is bad.'

Officer Grady: 'He crushed it into a little cube.'

Reporter: 'So if a member of the public sees this robot, what should they do?'

Officer Grady: 'First of all, keep away. This robot is dangerous. It has enormous strength. We believe it might have weapons . . .'

'He hasn't!' I shouted at the screen. 'All he wants is to do a bit of ironing and melt cheese!'

Officer Grady: 'Keep well away. Inform the police. We will act swiftly to decommission this bad machine.'

In case you didn't know what 'decommission' meant, they showed a clip of the crushing machine at R-U-Recycling chewing up mouthfuls of metal.

Reporter: 'Is there a reward for the capture of the rogue robot?'

Officer Grady: 'Yes – there will be a reward. A HUGE reward.'

He stared into the camera lens, right into the room, right over the beans on toast and into my heart, and said, 'And if we catch the person responsible, they will pay a heavy, heavy price.'

I dropped the empty beans tin . . .

into the recycling bin.

The DustUrchin said thank you and then did its

Mum impersonation. *'Hi, Alfie. Sorry I'm late again. Message me and let me know that you're all right. I've just heard about this business with the rampaging robot. The house has already updated me to say that you're home, but you know how I worry. Give me a call – I like to hear your voice. Go to bed and don't forget to say your prayers.'*

That night, I did remember to say my prayers. Or to think about them. Is it all right to pray for a robot? Praying for pets is controversial. It's debatable whether dogs and cats go to Heaven. It felt awkward asking God to help me save a robot. Especially one that was scaring people, smashing up police cars and interfering with their pizza deliveries. You don't want to put God in a difficult legal situation.

How could I keep Eric safe? I went to sleep thinking about what Dr Shilling had said about the planet Mars being entirely inhabited by robots. I imagined somehow taking Eric to Mars. I saw him in my mind, happily chatting to the other robots. Mars only has about a third of the mass of Earth, so he'd only weigh half as much. He could skip around doing ballet like D'Arcy, free from gravity and safe from all the people who wanted to destroy him.

STEP 16: SIX THOUSAND THREE HUNDRED AND TEN PARTS

When I got ready to leave the house next morning, the DustUrchin played me a message in Dr Shilling's voice. '*Don't forget. If you see the rogue robot, contact me immediately.*'

When I opened the front door, the house said, '*Have a good day, Alfie. Watch out for the rogue robot.*'

There was a message from Mum on my phone, '*Home in time for tea tonight. Keep in touch. Worried about rogue robot.*'

I passed the bus stop where a crowd of people were talking. I couldn't hear all they were saying, just odd words. Namely, the words 'massive', 'rampaging' and 'kidnapped a kid'. In the underpass, school kids' conversation echoed around the tunnel like a trapped bird.

Everyone was talking about Eric.

Nobody was saying anything good.

I went straight back to the hangar. I say 'straight back' – I took a detour at the end so that I wouldn't

pass too close to the house where I'd heard the weird noise. It seemed deader than ever in the daylight. How could there be an eye inside? Maybe it was just a pigeon or a rat?

Around the hangar, the brambles and nettles that Eric had trampled had sprung back up, as if they were under some kind of enchantment. I had to push through them to reach the entrance.

IT IS NOT POLITE TO ENTER A BUILDING WITHOUT AN INVITATION FROM THE OWNER.

'Eric!' I called. 'Is that you?'

DO COME IN.

In the morning light, it was surprisingly bright inside the hangar. A power shower of daylight was pouring in through that hole in the roof, splashing around on the broken wood and rusty tins, old springs and bits of wire and metal. I could see everything.

But I couldn't see Eric.

The tarpaulin I had hidden him under was bunched up in the middle of the floor.

How come I could hear him but not see him? He wasn't exactly easy to miss.

'Eric, where are you?'

I'M SORRY. I CAN'T ANSWER THAT QUESTION.

Then I saw him.

Not all of him. Just his head.

It was sitting on the windowsill, facing away from the tangle of brambles and nettles that covered the glass. It was not attached to the rest of his body.

Someone had decapitated Eric!

I gasped. 'Eric – where's the rest of you?'

He didn't answer, but something made me look down at my feet.

Have you ever sat near a baby in a high chair, and the baby is trying to eat its own dinner but keeps missing its mouth, so there is like a MOUNTAIN of Weetabix on the floor? Well, that's what the floor of the garage looked like. Or what it would have looked like if the baby had been eating electrical equipment instead of Weetabix and dropping bits of wire and screws and nuts and bolts instead of gloops of milky cereal mulch.

That's when I realized.

The mess on the floor –
was Eric.

Someone had taken him to pieces and scattered those pieces on the floor.

All except his head, perched on the windowsill, looking down at the mess that had once been his body.

I popped open my finger torch and scanned the floor, looking for something that was really Eric – something that wasn't just a nondescript scrap of metal. A mechanical brain or an electronic heart, perhaps. But there was nothing like that. Just a load of random components. Who could have done this?

I tried not to think too hard about that question because the first thing that popped into my head was the creature in the ruined house. The eye behind the letter box. What if they were still here, hiding in the shadows?

I tried to calm my imagination by concentrating on putting Eric back together again.

But where would I begin?

And if I did put him back together, would he be the same robot? Would he still be Eric?

Whatever, I wasn't going to leave him in pieces on the floor. My foot touched a metal jug with a thermostat inside. It looked like the kettle Eric used to make tea.

I looked for pieces that would fit into it. There was a kind of funnel, which must be where the water gets in. A box with some tea leaves in it. It took me ages to fit them together. Lefty has an inbuilt screwdriver hidden inside his thumb and a range of grips for holding things steady. I used my flesh-job hand to adjust my state-of-the-art fingers and tools. It felt like it had taken me hours to put together something that was really just a complicated tea-making machine.

Something moved.

Was it inside the shed or outside?

There was a faint tinkling sound.

I held my breath.

'Eric,' I whispered. 'Is that you?'

The tinkling sound stopped, then started again. It was Eric. He was trying to get a grip on his shivery rivets.

'Are you scared of something?' That was a worrying thought. Anything Eric was scared of must be really scary.

But Eric's rivets were not the only things that were shivering. The paint pots on the shelves were shaking like a row of little tin people desperately needing a wee. Spanners and screwdrivers hanging from a rack on the wall shook and chimed like little bells.

Something flashed past my head.

It hit Eric's chest and stuck there. A rusty old spanner – like the ones you use for fixing the seat of your bike. A paint pot tumbled by, dripping paint like a fat clumsy bird dripping poo. It landed on Eric's back and perched there like a tin parrot. A flock of screws whirled through the air and stuck to him like spiky measles. Keys and coins and a little metal pencil sharpener flew out of my pocket.

'Eric!' I yelled. 'You've gone magnetic. Stop it, before I get stabbed!'

I AM LOST.

The pile of splintered wood and metal in the middle of the floor – the stuff that had fallen from the ceiling when whatever it was crashed through it – moved.

Something was crawling underneath it.

I was staring at it, terrified, when something much bigger and noisier skidded past me along the floor. At first, I thought it was a bundle of clothes. Then it spoke.

'Make. It stop.'

It was Shatter.

She skidded across the floor. The metal in her new toes was attracted to Eric's magnetism. She clanged into Eric.

'Eric! Stop!'

Eric stopped shaking.

Metal objects stopped flying.

Shatter's leg hit the deck.

The pile of wood stopped moving.

D'Arcy and Tyler strolled in through the doorway.

'*You,*' I said. 'You did this. You killed Eric.'

'You can't kill. Something that. Isn't alive. It's a.

Machine. A rubbish. Machine by. The way. It has no. Weapons.'

'How did you find him?'

'Well—' began D'Arcy.

Shatter shut her up. 'Not your. Business. No. Need for you to. Know,' said Shatter.

'Why? Why did you do this to him?' I said, looking around at the mess on the floor.

'Revenge,' said Shatter, as though it was obvious.

'She wants to get her own back,' explained Tyler.

'I know what revenge means.'

'He dropped Shatila from a great height,' said Tyler. 'So she needs to get even.'

'He only did it because he thought she asked him to. He takes things literally.'

'Then on the news last night,' said D'Arcy, 'the police said there was going to be a reward. So we're going to turn him in for the money. I'm going to use the reward to fly to Moscow to see the Bolshoi Ballet. What about you, Tyler?'

I pointed out that they couldn't very well turn him in if he was in pieces.

'I think the. Head will do,' said Shatter.

I AM THE WORLD'S MOST SOPHISTI-CATED ROBOT.

Eric's disconnected head spoke. We all jumped in fright.

I HAVE SIX THOUSAND, THREE HUN-DRED AND TEN SEPARATE COMPO-NENTS . . .

'Oh, that was disturbing,' said D'Arcy.

'He's talking about how complicated he is,' said Tyler.

I said, 'He wants us to put him back together.'

I AM LOST.

They all jumped again.

By the time they calmed down, I was back on the floor, doing what I was doing before they'd turned up – namely fixing Eric. I never said anything. I never looked up. If they wanted to try to stop me, they could.

I spotted a washer, which seemed like it might fit round the kettle pipe. I went to pick it up, but couldn't get my finger under it. I tried adjusting one of Lefty's fingers so that I could flip it into my hand.

'Shatila doesn't want you to do that,' explained Tyler.

'In my. Country, people. Are blown to. Pieces all the time. And no. One cares. Why are you so. Bothered about a. Rubbish robot?'

'Shatila thinks,' said Tyler, 'you're too emotional.'

I didn't reply. I just slotted the metal washer into Lefty's Osprey Grip so that I could slide it into place. There was a horrible, gurgling, hiccoughy sound coming from somewhere in the room. I looked up.

Shatter's eyes were crinkled, and her face was red. She was biting the back of her own hand.

'Shatila,' explained Tyler, 'is laughing at you.'

That time, I actually did need a translation. You would never have thought that sound was a laugh.

'You can't even. Do Lego, so how. Are you. Going to fix. Him?'

'She thinks you can't even do quite simple things with your hand, so assembling something with over six thousand moving parts is really not going to happen, to be fair.'

I didn't look up because I was pretty sure there were tears in my eyes. If Lefty would just work properly, then I could do this easily. I didn't let them see, but I was trying everything I could to get my hand to listen to what my brain was saying. I tried visualizing its fingers opening and closing. I stormed the wrist with thoughts. I tried thinking about it. I tried not thinking about it. I tried so hard.

Still not looking up, I said, 'Tell you what, I'll try to fix him, and you sit there and laugh at me. Is that a deal?'

'Deal,' agreed Shatter. 'It is. Dead. Funny.'

'You mean we can just sit here and laugh while you fail?' said D'Arcy.

'Yes.'

'That actually does sound like fun.'

Shatter carried on laughing. The other two joined in.

There is one big difference between robots and humans:

Give a robot a job to do, and it will just get on and do it. It will carry on doing it until there's no more job left to do, or until it breaks down.

If a human says they're going to do something – for instance, laugh at my attempts to fix Eric – they will probably start OK, but then other stuff happens: Boredom, Distraction, Needing a Wee, or Wanting to Do Something Else Instead.

Shatter and her mates had decided that they would stand there and laugh at me while I worked on Eric. They made a decent start. They laughed a lot when I'd nearly fixed one entire hand, then dropped it, and all the fingers fell off and skittered away over the concrete. They also laughed fairly loudly when I dropped one of Eric's elbows, and it rolled under the chair. But I knew it would only be a matter of time before they wanted a change.

Tyler broke first.

When that elbow ball rolled under the chair, he rolled it back to me. He wasn't being kind. He was being bored. He wanted to watch the big silver ball rolling *more* than he wanted to watch me struggling. I rolled it back to him, just to see. He rolled it back again. I tried to pick it up with just my left hand. He came over and put it in Lefty's palm. Just then, I spotted the other elbow and asked him to pass it to me.

He glanced at Shatter. She glared at him. He didn't pass the elbow to me.

Then another plane flew overhead. So low, you could see the tread on its tyres. Shatter looked up at it.

'The Iberian Airways flight. From Barcelona,' she said, checking her watch. 'It's early.'

While Shatter was busy watching the plane, Tyler passed me the elbow. I said thanks, but he acted like he didn't know what I was talking about. I tried to fit the elbow on to the rest of the arm, but you had to get it at just the right angle. It must have been annoying to watch me struggling, because Tyler finally bent down and held it still for me.

I snapped back Lefty's thumb to reveal its hidden screwdriver-and-pliers combo.

'Your hand is impressive,' admitted Tyler, 'even if you can't work it properly.'

He carried on holding Eric's arm still while I tightened the nuts of his elbow joint with my thumb spanner.

Shatter got rattled when she saw what was going on. 'What's going on?' she said.

'I'm just doing this bit,' said Tyler. 'It's like Meccano.'

I used to love Meccano before my accident . . .'

There were holes in Eric's armour where the metal had splintered into tiny spikes, which would cut you if you brushed against them. Tyler used his metal fingers to just press them back into place.

'It's all about aligning the pieces,' he said. 'They went together once, so they should fit together again.'

I HAVE SIX THOUSAND, THREE HUN-DRED AND TEN SEPARATE COMPO-NENTS . . .

If you're watching someone do a jigsaw puzzle, there's no way you can stop your eye wandering around to see if you can spot the missing piece before they do. And if you do spot it then you want them to know about it. That's what was happening to D'Arcy.

'Look!' she whooped. 'There. I remember those braceletty things. They go round his ankles. Definitely.'

But when she bent down to pick them up, Shatter went off like a burglar alarm. 'Don't touch that!'

'I wasn't touching,' said D'Arcy. 'I was pointing.'

I picked them up and tried them. They fitted perfectly.

'They fit perfectly,' said D'Arcy.

'So,' said Shatter, 'what?'

But when Shatter looked up at the 10.40 KLM flight from Amsterdam as it roared by, D'Arcy started to help too.

Nearly all of Eric's insides were back together by then. They looked like a big copper squid lying on the floor surrounded by tentacles of rubber and wire. But with two steel arms.

'You know, I would hate to have to look at MY insides spread out on the floor,' said D'Arcy. 'Maybe we should turn his head round so he's looking the other way.'

I AM YOUR OBEDIENT SERVANT.

The feelings you get from putting someone's body back together while their head is talking to you from a nearby shelf are definitely complicated. Tyler – who had now started to translate for Eric as well as Shatter – said Eric was asking us if we wanted him to help.

'How?'

I KNOW HUNDREDS OF JOKES.

'That's a. Lie,' said Shatter. 'When we were. Taking him. Apart, he kept asking. If we would leave. Him alone if he told. Us jokes. But he didn't know any. Jokes.'

I winced. 'You're saying he was pleading for his life when you were taking him apart?'

She didn't answer that one.

'I wonder when this will start being him,' I said.

'What do you mean?'

'When will all this stuff on the floor start being Eric?'

'When we put his head back on, I suppose,' said D'Arcy.

I'd been thinking that Shatter would eventually give up and join in, but she just mooched around, poking about the place while we got on with fixing Eric.

When we were bolting on the big steel plates of his outer layer – his chest and the covers of his arms and legs – she looked down at us and snapped, 'What is he even. *For?* Robots are supposed. To have jobs and be. Shaped like their jobs. A pizza robot looks. Like an oven. A carpet-cleaner robot looks. Like a hedgehog. What does. He do? What is he. For?'

Then she turned round and walked out.

I looked at the other two to see if they would follow her, but they were totally focused on those plates.

'This is actually an exciting moment,' said D'Arcy.

Not going to lie – using Lefty to fasten them into place, I did feel a bit like a squire helping his knight put on his armour.

It took all three of us to get Eric's headless body to sit up. Eric's head was heavier than it looked; it needed two of us to lift it off the windowsill. I found a can of WD-40 on the ledge and used it to spray the threads round the base of his head. It didn't seem to need any screws or bolts. Mostly gravity kept it in place. That way, when they dropped the head into the neck, it could move from side to side.

Eric did look mighty. As soon as they saw the finished article, Tyler and D'Arcy wanted selfies.

D'Arcy sat back and looked around the hangar. 'We're like the Brotherhood without Banners,' she said, 'and this is our secret hideaway. Except when the wind whistles through then it's like Winterfell.'

Tyler translated this as, 'It gets cold.'

As soon as he said this, it started to get a bit warmer. Eric was making his hands glow and holding them up in front of us like a pair of five-fingered radiators.

'He's warming us up,' said Tyler, who had now taken to translating not just words but changes in temperature.

I pointed to the steam coming out of Eric's ears and explained that that meant he was also making tea.

'Oh,' cooed D'Arcy, 'he's a proper gentleman, isn't he?'

I HAVE SIX THOUSAND, THREE HUNDRED AND TEN SEPARATE COMPONENTS . . .

'We know,' said D'Arcy. 'We counted them.'

'We get bored sometimes,' explained Tyler.

'It's not actually true,' said D'Arcy. 'He's only got six thousand, three hundred and two.'

'We think the missing pieces,' said Tyler, 'are his leg.'

I HAVE SIX THOUSAND, THREE HUNDRED AND TEN SEPARATE COMPONENTS . . .

'I wish he wouldn't keep saying that.'

'Oh!' I said. 'Maybe he's trying to tell us something. Maybe there's a part missing.'

I opened my thumb torch and began to search the floor. I hadn't got far when the air filled with the sound of metal shivering again. Lefty was shivering. And D'Arcy's blades and Tyler's fingers. And the tins of paint on the shelves, and the tools hanging up on the shed wall.

'Keep back!' I shouted. 'Eric's going electromagnetic again! Eric! Don't do this!'

I AM YOUR OBEDIENT SERVANT.

Which is what Eric always says before totally ignoring me yet again.

At first, we were too hypnotized by what was happening on the floor to move. The pile of wood and plaster seemed to be growing, like a tiny, dusty volcano about to erupt.

Tyler gasped. 'What is that?'

'The Thing,' I said. 'The Thing that smashed through the roof years ago.'

Something barged the wood aside as the Thing

shoved itself clear of the rubbish. It shook the mud and sawdust off itself as it rose into the beam of my finger torch.

I suddenly realized what it was. I turned to the other two to tell them, but they had vanished.

The minute the Thing rose up out of the pile of scrap, they had run away. They never saw what it was that Eric's electromagnetic field had hauled up out of the ground.

It was Eric's missing leg.

STEP 17: AT YOUR SERVICE

Imagine if Cinderella's entire leg had fallen off instead of just her glass slipper. Imagine how good the prince would have felt if he'd strolled into her kitchen with the whole leg under his arm – and stuck it back on. That's how I felt as I hauled the leg out from under the rubbish and took it over to Eric. I twisted Eric's scooter-leg substitute out of its slot and put it to one side. Then I knelt down in front of Eric, just like Prince Charming – if Cinderella had been a six-foot-six man of steel with four spring-loaded retaining clips inside her hip.

The clips were stiff. I doused them with WD-40. The clips slotted neatly over the four toggles inside Eric's leg.

There were no Prince Charming fireworks, no Cinderella dancing, but it did feel magical when the last clip clicked. The moment it did, the leg kicked out. If I'd been a few centimetres to the left, it would have kicked me clear through the window. Eric's eyes glowed as he looked down at his own leg.

'Got to say,' I said, standing back to admire it, 'that is definitely your leg.'

Eric didn't just stand up, he AROSE.

He placed his two feet side by side and put his hands on the floor. Then he levered himself upright. Inside his body, cogs cranked, springs pinged and metal rang – as if there was a factory starting up within.

Outside, wobbling around on a scooter, Eric had looked big.

Inside, with his own two feet planted on the hangar floor, and his head reaching up towards the hole in the roof, he looked monumental.

I really wished the others had not run off and could see him now.

WHAT DO SEA MONSTERS EAT? said Eric.

'Not this again.'

FISH AND SHIPS. THE JOKE IS NOW CORRECT.

'That actually is a joke. Eric, you told a joke.'

HA HA.

Seeing Eric standing there all put back together and complete reminded me of something Dr Shilling had said about muscle memory – how we store some of our memory not in our brains, but in our hands and arms.

'Maybe some of your memory is in your leg.'

MY NAME IS ERIC. I AM LOST . . .

He was looking around the hangar again, eyes blazing, as if he was trying to find something.

'You knew your leg was here, didn't you? That's why you brought me here. What are you looking for now?'

Eric ignored me completely. He pushed his right leg forward. And, just like when you walk, his left arm and his shoulder slightly swung forward to balance him out. Then . . . remember what Dr Shilling said about walking being a series of narrowly avoided falls? That describes exactly what happened to Eric next.

Except for the 'narrowly avoided' bit.

He brought his left leg forward, but his right arm and shoulder didn't swing forward this time. They went the other way. Like his top half and his bottom half were having a terrible argument. He toppled forwards with such a metal racket anyone outside must've thought it was raining buckets and baths. I was expecting the whole of Skyways to come running to see what the noise was.

This was not the first time Eric had almost demolished me. His huge arm smashed against some metal shelving. He slammed into the floor right next to me, and I swear the floor bounced. The rebound threw me up into the air so violently that I collided with a set of shelves that was coming the other way.

Then I hit the floor.

Then the shelves hit me.

They lay so heavily across my chest, I could barely breathe.

A strange, cackling sound echoed in the air. As though someone was laughing.

I wasn't laughing.

Neither was Eric.

It seemed like the air was laughing.

I said, 'Help! Get these off me.'

No one answered. That's when I remembered D'Arcy and Tyler had run off in fright.

'Hello?' I called. 'Help?'

But there was no one there to help me. I thought I could phone someone for assistance, but found that my phone had skittered away out of reach when I fell.

I was trapped.

And alone.

I wedged Lefty under the shelves. A normal hand would have hurt, but Lefty knew no pain. I locked his fingers together and used him to lever the shelves off my chest. They shifted just a little.

Then they shifted a lot. Something swept them off me as though they were made of snow. I wasn't alone at all. Eric was taking care of me.

'Thanks, Eric,' I said.

I AM AT YOUR SERVICE. ALWAYS.

He looked at his own hand as he said that, as if he expected himself to be holding something.

I went over and picked up my phone. It was popping with news alerts about the rogue robot.

'Eric,' I said, 'I think we should get out of here. Can you try to walk again?'

He slid one foot forward and crashed to the floor once more. This time, he landed on his back. He looked quite comfortable. I told him to power down.

'Sleep well, Eric,' I said. 'We'll sort out the walking tomorrow.'

It was getting dark again when I left the hangar. I tried to keep as far away from the spooky end of the building as possible, keeping the trees between me and its windows because it always felt like they were watching me.

Even so, I still heard the door creak open.

And then I heard a voice shout, 'Alfie Miles!'

And then I ran and ran and kept running till I got home.

STEP 18: HOME

'*Good afternoon, Alfie. Your heartbeat is raised again,*' said the house. '*Why not sit down while I put the kettle on.*'

I stepped into the hallway.

'Alfie?'

At first, I thought it was the DustUrchin talking. Then I smelt spices and onions frying, and I knew Mum was home and making a curry.

We sat down at the table to eat it. She told me all about her day. I didn't tell her anything about mine.

Later on, when we were clearing up, I noticed a photo on one of the bookshelves. It was of a toddler standing between two big people. Each big person was holding one of the toddler's hands. The toddler had a grin on his face as wide as his head. He looked like he was crashing through the finishing line of the Toddler Olympics.

I was still staring at it when Mum came up behind me.

'What're you looking at?'

189

'I was trying to remember learning to walk.'

'Oh. Most people don't remember that. Are you trying to remember something else? Does this picture remind you of anything?'

'Not really.' It was just a photo. Probably I was the toddler and the big people were Mum and maybe one of my big cousins. 'I was just wondering how long it takes a baby to learn to walk.'

'Depends on the baby. Usually babies are starting to walk by the time they're one. Babies learn so much in that first year – how to talk, how to recognize people, how to walk. Is there something at the edge of your mind, something you're trying to focus on? Are you sure you're OK, Alfie?'

'How do they learn?'

'Who? Babies? Mostly it just happens, but you need a bit of help at the end. No one learns to walk without a bit of help. Is that all you wanted to know?'

She sounded disappointed.

'Yes,' I said. 'Thanks.'

Of course, no one can walk unless someone teaches them! I could teach Eric to walk. Can robots learn? Of course they can. The DustUrchin had learned which were the really dirty corners of the house. If a vacuum cleaner can learn, surely a giant mechanical knight could.

I was so motivated by this idea that I ran upstairs

and started to google everything I could think of about walking. Then I thought, Why am I doing this? I know someone who has learned to walk twice. Once when she was little and once when she lost one of her feet and had to start again. She must be some kind of world expert on learning to walk.

Shatter.

I messaged her to ask her to meet me the next day at the hangar.

No. Body, she messaged back, *tells me where. To go.*

Fair enough, I thought. But I bet you turn up just the same.

STEP 19: WHY WOULD I. EVER HELP YOU?

Shatter was waiting for me. I knew she would be.

'What is it you. Want?' she said.

'Eric's got two legs. We could teach him to walk.'

'Why would I. Ever. Help you?'

'You wouldn't be helping me. You'd be helping Eric.'

'Why would I want. To help an over. Grown tea-making thing? Are you trying. To be nice to. Me because you're scared. That I will bully. You because you nicked my. Mates?'

'I didn't nick your mates. They just helped because it was fun. It IS fun. If you helped me, I bet it would be fun.'

'I'm not interested in. Fun,' she said, and walked out.

A plane passed overhead so low that all the brambles in the doorway shook.

Then Shatter strode right back in. I thought she was going to tell me where the plane was going. Instead she scrambled up on to one of the fallen shelves – she really is good on her state-of-the-art foot – and started messing about with some kind of plastic box on the wall.

'Shine your finger. On here.'

I pointed the finger torch at the box. She flipped it open. There was a row of switches inside.

'Fuses,' she said. 'This one. Has tripped.'

She flicked the switch and *BLAM!*

A bomb of light exploded around us. Colours and shapes bounced around me. Dented paint tins, broken shelves, smashed floorboards, spiders' webs and, most of all, Eric, lying on the ground like a giant angel.

Shatter had fixed the lights. They were so bright it made you feel as though everyone in the world could see you.

'How did you know about that?'

'When you were. All playing robots, I had a proper. Look around the place.'

She tugged a piece of string that was hanging down from the ceiling like a light pull and told me to stand back. When she pulled it, an entire table lowered itself down from the ceiling. Its legs popped out as it came into land. The table was made of metal with rulers engraved on its edges. We use our kitchen table for chopping veg and making pies. This one looked like it was meant for building jumbo jets.

'This,' I said, 'is unusual. Why did they have a table in the ceiling?'

'To save. Space,' said Shatter. 'That's why they

called. It the Space Age. Let's. Start. Do you. Have a manual?'

'A manual for Eric? No.'

'Did you look for. One. Online?'

'That's the weird thing. I've spent ages looking at stuff about robots. I've never come across anything like Eric. There's nothing about him on the whole internet.'

'Maybe he's from. The Future.'

'Maybe he's from space,' I said, looking up at the legendary hole in the roof.

'We. Are going to need a. Screwdriver.'

'There's one in my thumb,' I said, snapping it back.

'Let's try these. Drawers too,' said Shatter.

The hangar had big drawers on either side, crammed with nothing but screwdrivers – big, little, tiny, cross-top, flat-top, electrical, adjustable – every type of screwdriver you could imagine. Plus spanners and wrenches, pliers and wire cutters.

It turns out that Shatter really is a world-class expert on learning to walk. On her phone, she showed me clips of films the scientist Eadweard Muybridge made years ago. He took loads of photographs of animals and humans walking, and then made them into little films (which looked like flickery gifs) so that people could really study what was happening when a horse ran, or a boy walked.

Shatter explained that human beings learn to walk in stages. Such as crawling, bum shuffling, holding on to furniture.

'We could take Eric through all those phases,' I said, 'but in a single morning.'

Neither of us really wanted to wake Eric to start with. It's a strange thing, but Eric never looked more like a human being than he did when he was lying on the floor of that hangar asleep. We actually whispered in case we woke him, like you do with a baby.

Shatter spotted that his ankle bracelets were loose. 'That's why his feet. Are dragging. If he lifts them up. They just flop down. That's never going to. Work. Give me a hand. Literally.'

'You mean . . .'

'Take your hand. Off and let me look inside. If we are. Going to make him. Walk, we. Need to know how. Muscles and tendons and nerves and everything work.'

I know it sounds weird. It's not like I didn't know there were circuits and chips inside Lefty. But seeing them sticking out all over the place made me feel unbalanced. When Shatter started poking around inside – not gonna lie – I felt queasy.

Shatter found this interesting. 'You can feel. In your real. Arm when I touch your. Fake hand?'

'It's not a fake hand. It's a real hand. It's just not made of flesh.'

'But you can. Feel it?'

'No,' I said. 'I don't have detachable nerve endings.'

It was true. I couldn't feel any pain. But I was feeling *something*: confusion, maybe; embarrassment, a bit; but, most of all, I just wanted my hand back.

She picked up the screwdriver. I couldn't help it. I screwed up my eyes as if I was waiting for an injection. She jabbed the screwdriver into Lefty's thumb. I jumped. She laughed.

'Can I have my hand back now?'

She tossed me back my hand. 'It's easy,' she said. 'Fingers are like. Puppets. They have. Strings. The. Strings all join. Up in the wrist. Pass me the soldering iron."

We decided to make all the hardware adjustments while Eric was in sleep mode. The more awkward and complicated things seemed to be, the more useful Lefty's integral tools turned out to be. I was learning as much about my new hand as I was about Eric.

Then it was time to wake him up.

'OK, Eric,' I said. 'Let's get you up on your feet so that you can walk out of here . . . Arise, Sir Eric.'

And Eric arose.

He placed his hands on either side of his body. He pushed himself up. Blue flames flowed down his arms and crackled over his joints.

'Eric, are you OK?' I said.

Every move he made flashed and sparked. He was a lightning storm with his legs. I backed away.

He was standing on his own two feet. He thrust his hand into the air and roared:

I AM SIR ERIC. AND NOW MY QUEST BEGINS!

He sounded pretty pleased with himself. He moved one leg towards me. Wobbled. Steadied himself. He looked like he was going to move the next one.

'Whoa, steady,' said Shatter. 'Steady, Eric. Get used to standing. Up first. Keep it. Nice and slow.'

Straight away, the fire and lightning stopped. It seemed as though he was sucking all that energy back inside himself, trying to concentrate on keeping his balance.

I AM YOUR OBEDIENT SERVANT.

'Sometimes, I think a word,' I said, 'can trigger his memory. Like when I said "armour", he started to talk like a knight. Maybe if we just said, "Walk, Eric", then just walking could be his quest.'

He stayed still, but tense like someone on the edge of a diving board, getting ready to take the plunge. Like he was considering his options. In my mind I seemed to see all the different ways there are of walking. Shatter swings her arms like a boxer swaggering into the ring. D'Arcy's blades make her bounce slightly, like someone walking on the moon. Tyler walks with his head down, as though he's looking for something. Everyone's walk is different. I wondered what Eric's walk would be like.

It was like an earthquake.

The floor groaned for mercy wherever he planted his massive feet. Chunks of the ceiling fell in his wake.

Shatter and I hurried after him, like when a mum or dad runs after a kid who has just learned to ride a bike. He kept going. He was way better than any of the robots you'll ever see on YouTube.

Eric could actually definitely and completely walk.

It's a pity that he used that skill by walking AWAY. But we'll get to that later.

The point is we did it.

We taught Eric to walk.

'He's going. Out. Side,' said Shatter.

It was true. Just like on the day he brought me here, he seemed to know where he was going, like he was looking for something.

I AM LOST.

Eric sounded more like a Marvel superhero announcing his name than a robot lost in an airport.

He stepped up towards where the broken door still lay on the floor. He put his foot on it. He lost his balance. He was going to fall.

I ran to him.

I grabbed his hand.

I held it tight.

With Lefty. Without me even thinking about it – without even trying – I had closed the fingers of my state-of-the-art hand around Eric's fingers. Lefty had come to life. He was part of me at last. I was holding hands just like the toddler-me in the photograph.

That's when I remembered.

Holding someone's hand had triggered my memory, and in my mind, I saw . . .

You.

STEP 20: YOU

Memories bulleted through my brain. Some of them were too fast to catch, but one exploded like grenade.

The accident.

I remembered that it wasn't just my accident. Someone else got hurt.

You.

I let go of Eric's hand. Just like I must have let go of your hand on that day.

Eric must have said something, but I wasn't listening. I ran out into the woods and kept running until I got home.

Mum was at the front door. I stopped in front of her.

'Mum . . .' I said.

I didn't need to say any more. She could tell just by looking at me.

'Ah,' she said, taking my hand. 'You've remembered, haven't you?' She led me into the kitchen and made me sit down. 'Take your time,' she said. 'I've waited for this to happen for so long. I can wait a bit longer.'

Words and pictures and feelings were still streaming into my brain. Sometimes, they'd stop as if they were buffering. Sometimes, they'd torrent into my head like a super-fast download.

It was you.

I'd finally remembered you.

My little brother, Arty.

How could I have completely forgotten about my own brother?

'Mum, where's Arty?'

This time, I was the one who didn't have to wait to hear. Asking that question was like clicking 'open' on a zip file . . .

A bus is coming down the road.

I'm holding your hand. You're on your scooter. It was a really sunny day. We'd been up to the shops at the Circus. You want to dash out into the road. It's a game. The buses stop and back up if anyone runs in front of them. It's in their programming. So they are totally one hundred per cent safe. The bus stops. You wave at it, and it flashes its lights at you. Every kid loves that. Everyone is always doing it, just to see the lights go. I yank you backwards on to the pavement.

'That,' I said, 'is reckless.'

'I'm big four,' you said.

You thought being four years old meant you were indestructible.

I held you back. We were going home. We'd been scootering down the underpass. You loved the underpass because the ramp made the scooter go fast, and the tunnel because it made your screams go loud.

The bus goes by. Nothing else is coming, so we step into the road. Someone must have stepped in front of the bus after it went by, though, because it stopped. Then it backed into us.

The picture goes a bit fuzzy after that.

I remember my hand in the road and not being able to figure out how it got there. I don't remember any pain. I remember lots of fear. You were lying in the road. It didn't look like there was anything wrong with you. You were perfect. No bruises or cuts. Not in my memory anyway. It looked like you were asleep.

The bus just drove itself away. It left you lying in the road. And me kneeling next to you . . .

'Mum,' I said, 'is Arty . . .'

'He's in hospital. I sit with him every day as soon as I finish work.'

Other thoughts and memories shot into my brain after that. Like the fact that Mum was normally nearly always there. We always did stuff together. Went places. The three of us. For weeks and weeks, I'd been mostly on my own. I'd never normally have got away with going to the airport all on my own. Mum had been missing.

'Come on,' she said. 'It's time you came with me.'

STEP 21: IN YOUR FACE, DESCARTES

Hundreds of years ago, there was a philosopher in France called René Descartes. He went to see one of those mechanical dolls I'd seen when I'd been searching online for Eric. I think it was the one that could play the flute. Or maybe the one that could poo. Anyway, he did some philosophy about it and decided that humans were just robots with extra features. Their hearts and livers and kidneys were just a squishier kind of clockwork. Humans just did what they were programmed to do.

He used to look out of his window in Holland at all the people rushing off to work and school and think, *How can you tell that they are people and not just robots with hats and coats on?*

I'm not a French philosopher. But I do know Descartes was wrong. There's one big difference between robots and people.

If a robot falls apart, you can put it back together again with a screwdriver and some duct tape. If its brain stops working, you can reboot it. If it loses its

memory, you can reload it from the Cloud. If all that doesn't work, you can call the helpline.

In your face, Descartes. People are nothing like machines.

STEP 22: PEOPLE ARE NOTHING LIKE MACHINES

Mum tried to keep cheerful as we walked along the hospital corridor. A cleaner bot was working its way towards us, polishing the floor.

'Look!' Mum said. 'A Tiggy-Winkle. That's the same as our DustUrchin, but it has polishing skills too. I'd love one of those.'

'*Happy anniversary of the invention of the television,*' said the Tiggy-Winkle for something to say.

'Thank you,' said Mum.

A few seconds later, Father Mangan came round the corner. He's our parish priest, but he also does all the priest-things that need to be done in the hospital.

He's good, but his suits are always too big for him – like he has shrunk in the wash, but his clothes haven't.

'Alfie!' he said. 'We don't see you here very often.' He put his hand out to shake mine. He had to pull his suit sleeve up a bit to get enough of his hand out to shake.

'How's your hand?' he said.

I held it up for him to see.

'State of the art,' he said. 'You look well. When you think . . .'

He looked at Mum. She nodded. There were more holes in this conversation than in a cheese grater.

'It gives you hope,' he said.

Mum nodded again.

'I've just been in to see Arty,' he said.

Mum looked worried.

'I was just passing. We had a nice chat. Well, I did the talking. We have to have faith that he can hear us. The more you talk to him, the easier it is to believe, eh?'

'Yes,' said Mum.

'Well, I'm around all morning, if I can help at all. Keep believing, eh?'

Once he'd gone, I said, 'Why would I think Arty couldn't hear me?'

Mum didn't answer.

STEP 23: ARTY IS MISSING

Arty is missing. We know where his body is – on a bed in the HDU, hooked up to three different drips: one for nutrition, one for hydration and one for medicine.

But we don't know where Arty is.

If you want a description – he has thick curly black hair. He never ever walks, but always runs.

We don't know where that Arty is.

We know where Arty's favourite things are because the doctors told Mum to bring his favourite things in and put them round his bed to make it feel more like home. There are his plastic jousting knights, his toy cars and action figures. The 'dragon' is actually an educational toy chameleon.

We don't know where Arty is.

Where are you, Arty?

There were wires clipped on your fingers and taped to your chest, connecting you to machines to measure your breathing, your heartbeat, your brain activity. Monitors were beeping and blipping.

You really are part boy, part machine. Much more like Wolverine than me.

The bed was jacked up at an angle so that your eyes would have been staring straight ahead, if they'd been open. But they hadn't been open for ages.

Mum told me to say hello to you and believe that you could hear me.

'Hello,' I said.

One of the monitors beeped, and the graph on its screen jumped in jagged peaks.

'Wow,' said the nurse who was checking Arty over. 'He's really pleased to hear you, isn't he?'

I looked at Mum. She smiled and nodded, but when the nurse had gone, she said, 'It does that sometimes. I just don't know if it's true. But do keep talking.'

'What about?'

'I know. That's the hard thing.'

Your head was in a kind of brace. That was to keep your brain safe. I thought about what Dr Shilling had said about the head not being the safest place to keep the brain. I wished I could lift your brain out and put it in the safest place in the house.

Mum was telling me about how she talked to you every day.

'But you do run out of things to say after a while,' she whispered. 'I start by telling him what I did the day before. But if all I did the day before was sit in a plastic chair talking to him, well, that doesn't leave you with much to say, does it, Arty? Come on, Arty: one blink for *yes*; two blinks for *no*?'

I tried to start talking to you. But it was only when Mum went off to talk to the doctors that I really got going. Because it was only then that I started to talk about Eric. It might be controversial, but it felt good. Just me and you knowing about him.

I kept watching the heart monitor. It went up and down all the time, but I was nearly definitely sure that it went higher during the funny bits and during the scary bits. I slightly exaggerated a bit sometimes to make the funny bits funnier, and the scary bits scarier. The more I did it, the higher the peaks were.

A very small doctor in a very bright hijab came in to do some tests on you. She glanced at the brain monitor. 'Wow! That was a good conversation! Look at those peaks and troughs. It's called the attention differential. You should definitely come again.'

'I'll come every day,' I said.

'Did you enjoy your big brother's story, Arty? One blink for *yes*. Two blinks for *no*.'

No blink.

'How about squeezing my hand, then?'

No squeeze.

She pulled the curtains around your bed and told me and Mum to go and wait in the atrium. There's a play slide there shaped like a dragon with big eyelashes and a cherry-red smile. There are mountains and rainbows painted on the wall behind it. No one was playing on it just then. I was thinking how much you would love it.

There were a couple of couches, a coffee machine and a big window with a view towards the airport. No one was looking out of the window because there was also a telly in there with a screen so big you felt like you might fall into it. The sound was switched off, and for some reason this made it really hard to look away from. My eyes were hypnotized by a programme about people who restore vintage cars. But my brain was only thinking about you.

I knew I'd forgotten some big, important things,

but I'd always thought that thing was the accident. How could I have forgotten *you*?

'Why didn't you tell me?'

'I wanted to,' said Mum. 'I really wanted to. But the doctors said give it time; it will all come back. The mind needs time to recover just like your body does. You had enough to cope with accepting that you'd lost a hand without having to think about Arty.'

'That's why you were always late from work. You were coming here. On your own.'

'I did think that, in the end, you would start to wonder.'

'And the room – Arty's room.'

'You never went near it. It was like you couldn't even see it.'

Now all kinds of memories of you were torrenting. Memories of you running around everywhere, pretending you were riding a horse—

Oh my days – I've just thought. That Lego that Mum put out for me to practise with – that's *your* Lego, isn't it? And the scooter I used for Eric's leg – that's *your* scooter. And the photograph of the toddler learning to walk – that's *you* in the middle of that photograph, not me. I am in the photograph. It's me – not a big cousin – holding your hand.

I'm your big brother. I'm supposed to look out for you.

Mum said, 'You OK, Alfie?'

'Mum,' I said, 'tell me something. The accident – was it my fault?'

'No, Alfie. Nothing to do with you.'

'So, will Arty be OK?'

'Let's talk about it later, shall we?'

She didn't look at me when she said that. I knew she was keeping something from me. Something my brain didn't want to let in. Like maybe it wasn't exactly my fault, but maybe there was something I could or should have done that might have saved you.

Mum guessed what I was thinking about.

'It wasn't your fault,' she said.

Her eyes were unusually shiny. At first, I thought it was just the reflection of the telly, but when I turned round to check there were actual tears coming out of her eyes.

I'd never seen Mum cry before. She must have done a lot of private crying since the accident. I had no idea what to say, so I shuffled up and gave her hand a squeeze. She looked down at our hands.

'Alfie,' she said, 'you – you just squeezed my hand.'

'Sorry.'

'With Lefty! You squeezed my hand with Lefty. You've finally learned to use your hand. Alfie, that's amazing.'

She squeezed back. I swear I could feel that squeeze all the way up in my brain.

On the way out, we met another doctor in the lift. She asked if I was your brother and said she'd heard a lot about me. 'But no one,' she said, 'told me what a great storyteller you are.'

'How's that?' said Mum.

'He was excited to hear your voice, Alfie, and the story just kept the ball up there. I'll show you.'

She tipped her tablet towards us. There was a graph on the screen that looked like a cross-section of the spikiest mountain range in the world.

'These peaks,' she said, 'are when Arty's brain is most active. Look here. All these peaks bunched together, that's when Alfie was talking to him.'

'So . . . he really can hear us?' said Mum.

'He's in there somewhere,' said the doctor. 'And he likes to hear his brother's stories.'

I thought Mum was going to cry again.

'It's been so hard talking to him,' she said, 'when you don't know if he can really hear. But now . . . Oh, thank you, Alfie.'

'What were you talking to him about, if you don't mind my asking?' said the doctor. 'Must have been thrilling stuff.'

'Oh, just stuff.'

'What kind of stuff?'

'Stuff I did. With a friend of mine.'

The lift stopped.

'This is my floor,' she said, and stepped out. 'Don't forget, Alfie – keep telling the stories.'

It was thinking about that graph on the doctor's tablet that gave me the idea. That's when I thought – if holding Eric's hand woke my memories, maybe if *you* could hold Eric's hand it would wake you too.

I don't know if the accident was my fault. But I do know that I can do my best to make you better, Arty. Because I've got something better than just a story. I've got the *real thing*.

I've got Eric.

STEP 24: EMERGENCY SITUATION

The driverless shuttle is supposed to go non-stop to Concorde Circus, but just before the estate entrance the bus said, *'Due to the current emergency situation, we are being held here. Please continue your journey by other means.'*

'What emergency situation?' said Mum.

It turned out that the Emergency Situation was Eric.

We got off the bus and started walking home to Stealth Street. All the way up B–52 Street and right round on to Hurricane Way, the streets were full of people and robots. There were people standing in doorways looking up and down the road. Robots of every kind – Pizzabots, lawnmowers, street cleaners – were toddling along the pavements.

'What,' said Mum, 'is going on?'

'News Update,' said a passing DustHog. *'The rogue robot has been located and confined to Concorde Circus on the Skyways estate.'*

When I heard that, my heart sank.

Now that Eric could walk, he couldn't stop. While I was at the hospital talking to you, he was probably stomping all over the place in plain sight.

A police siren blared once, then stopped – *blam!* – as if someone had stamped on it. I found out a bit later that that was because Eric had.

We followed the crowd to Concorde Circus. There was a ring of police cars right round the traffic island. I couldn't see Eric at first because of the crowd and the tree. Then he stomped into view. He was standing on the bonnet of one of the police cars. He put one foot on the roof. The roof sagged under his weight. The windscreen buckled and shattered. Eric made a giant stride off the roof of that car, on to the next one.

And the next one.

And the next one.

Roofs bent, and windscreens shattered everywhere he went. He did a full lap of the Circus, leaving a trail of destruction behind him. He didn't mean to leave a trail of destruction. He'd just got a bit happy about his newly-recovered walking skills. All around the Circus, there were people holding up their phones, live-streaming Eric.

Eric took this as a sign that everyone loved him. He waved at the crowd. Bowed his head and said:

IT IS CONSIDERED POLITE TO STAND FOR THE NATIONAL ANTHEM.

Which was unnecessary, as they were already standing up. When he started singing, they covered their ears. Some of them ran away.

A van pulled up. Rusty got out, carrying the flame cutter. 'It's OK, everyone!' he shouted as the police cleared a way through the crowd for him. 'You won't believe the mix I've got here. So hot. Any minute now, this robot will be a neat pile of conveniently sized metal squares.'

As he walked towards Eric, the flame at the end of his metal cutter sparked and hissed like a blazing blue snake. Eric had no idea he was in trouble. He bowed his head and said:

I AM YOUR OBEDIENT SERVANT.

Rusty lowered his visor and walked towards Eric. He turned to the crowd and said, 'Would anyone like to give me a hand?'

You know what happened next. Eric scanned the faces of the crowd, barged through the barrier of police cars and grabbed me.

Mum screamed.

Everyone screamed.

'Alfie! Run!' yelled Mum.

Eric took two giant strides towards me. I grabbed his outstretched hand. He swung me up above the crowd.

'No!' yelled Mum. 'Help! It's stealing my son!'

'It's OK, Mum!' I yelled. 'We're friends!'

She couldn't hear over all the screaming and yelling. Eric plonked me down in front of Rusty.

'You asked him for a hand,' I explained, taking off Lefty for him to see. 'He takes things pretty literally.'

I honestly thought Rusty would recognize me, but he didn't. He just rolled his eyes.

'Why would I need some little kid's fake hand?'

'My hand,' I said, 'is not fake. Just because a hand is

not made of flesh, does not mean it's not real. Lefty is a state-of-the-art hand, and he can do stuff your hand can't. For instance, this . . .'

I reached up, and with my flame-retardant, heat-resistant fingers, I pinched the burning end of the metal cutter. Because it was so hot, the metal was surprisingly soft. I squeezed it until I'd nipped the end of the tube shut and snuffed out the flame.

When his flame went out, Rusty's face lit up. 'What did you do that for? Well, just you wait. Now sparks really are going to FLY!'

Rusty shouted that last word very loud indeed.

And Eric took it very literally indeed.

He put me under his arm. He began to shake.

Then the ground began to shake.

There was a bang.

Some smoke.

And Eric left the ground.

He rose into the air like the biggest football trophy ever being lifted by a colossal invisible footballer. For as far as you could see, every face and every phone tipped up to watch us as we pushed higher and higher. Twigs and branches snapped and leaves whirled as we snagged against the tree. Gasps and screams blew by like lost party balloons. I tried to pick Mum's face out in the crowd below.

'Eric, take me to the hospital!' I yelled.

So, Arty, you're probably thinking he's about to walk into the room, and you're going to meet him in the flesh. Well, not the flesh, but the metal.

Are you excited? Can you even wait?

Well, you'll have to wait.

Because the truth is, he's not here.

Not going to lie, Arty. I've been making it up. There isn't really an Eric-based emergency situation. I made all this up to try to wake you. I thought if I told you something unbelievably exciting it might make you open your eyes. It didn't work. I think somehow you must have known that none of it was true.

STEP 25: ROBOT REVOLUTION

This is what *really* happened when Mum and I left the hospital that night.

We caught the shuttle bus back to Stealth Street. We didn't see an Eric-related riot. The DustHog came up and said, '*If you liked the news about the rogue robot, you'll love the news that is streaming right now.*'

So we watched the news at home as we had our tea.

'Oh! That's Dr Shilling!' said Mum, all excited. 'Look! Your Dr Shilling.'

The news reporter was asking her about Eric . . .

Reporter: '*The rogue robot that has been terrorizing the Skyways estate has alarmed a lot of people. Is it the first of many? Are robots fed up of bringing us pizzas and emptying our bins? Are we facing a robot revolution? Is this the beginning of a robot war?*'

Dr Shilling: '*No.*'

Reporter: '*There's always been a rumour in the Skyways area that, back in the day, your family – the Shilling family – built a warrior robot who went mad and killed someone with a sword. Is this robot possibly that crazed warrior robot come back to life?'*

Dr Shilling: '*No.'*

Reporter: '*How can you be so sure?'*

Dr Shilling: '*First, there never was a warrior robot. My family helped children who had been injured in accidents and wars. Second, robots do not go mad. Because robots do not have minds. Robots only do what they're told to do. Robots are not pets. Robots are not replacement people. Robots are machines that do jobs. Robots shaped like people confuse our emotions. We want to be their friends, to get close to them. And if that happens tragedy can follow. Because they are not our friends.'*

Reporter: '*So there never was a Shilling robot?'*

Dr Shilling: *Looks uncomfortable* '*There WAS a robot. And that robot was involved in a terrible tragedy. An air crash. But that was a very long time ago. When my father was a little boy. And the robot was destroyed in the crash. If you're saying that Eric could have survived the crash, well, that seems impossible.'*

Reporter: '*Eric?'*

Dr Shilling: *Glares at the reporter* '*That robot was called Eric. This robot is an unlicensed robot built by someone very irresponsible who should be brought to justice.'*

'They do say,' said Mum, 'careful what you wish for.'
I looked at her. 'What do you mean?'

224

'Robots can do terrible things with the best of intentions. Like the magic cod fish.'

'What magic cod fish?'

'The story goes,' said Mum, 'that, long ago, a fisherman caught a magic cod fish. The cod fish offered him three wishes if he would just throw him back in the sea. The fisherman's first wish was to see his son come back from the war. The second was for a hundred pieces of gold. He didn't, he said, even need a third wish.

'The magic cod fish granted his wishes. But the cod fish didn't understand all the other things about being a human and being a dad. So he brought the fisherman's son home from the war – in a coffin. And the king sent a hundred gold pieces in recognition of the son's heroic death. Robots are all a bit like magic cod fish. You have to be very careful how you talk to them.'

I had one wish for Eric, I thought. I wanted him to walk into your room and say something – anything – in his ice-cream-van-playing-bagpipes voice. If I could just make that happen, I knew you would sit up in the bed and say, 'Alfie!'

There's nothing complicated about that wish, is there? I mean, what could go wrong with a wish like that?

*

So next morning, first thing, I went back to the hangar.

There was no sign of Eric. Just a vast empty space full of cobwebs and dust, with a big round table suspended from the ceiling, swaying gently in the breeze.

I listened.

Nothing but a blackbird singing, and – through the trees – the sounds of the airport.

I searched every corner with my thumb torch. The only thing I found was your scooter. If I hadn't found that, I might have thought the whole thing had been a dream. I tucked it under my arm to take home, because you're going to need it when you get better.

I went back outside to start searching the woods. Surely Eric would be easy to track. A man of steel is bound to leave footprints.

Nothing. No sign.

If he hadn't gone off through the woods, where had he gone? There was only one place left to look: the spooky outhouse.

I tip-toed through the long grass. The door was slightly ajar. I pushed it gently. It swung open. A cloud of dust swirled out of the room beyond. Something touched my hair. I jumped back. It was just flakes of dry paint pattering down from the lintel on to my head. I leaned into the room. A spider's web as big and heavy as a Christmas stocking hung down from the light fitting. In the corner, a set of broken steps led up to a balcony covered in stacks of yellow paper. Something – maybe a mouse – was scrabbling about among them.

Whatever or whoever it was knew about Eric.

I was scared. But I was going to find them.

I stepped in.

A stack of yellow paper slumped over and crashed to the floor. Sheets flew like skeleton bats around the room.

'Who's there?' I said calmly. OK, so I probably screamed.

'Where have. You been?' asked Shatter.

'What are you doing here?'

'I always come. Here. I was coming. Here before you found Eric. I was watching the. Day you hid. Him here.'

'And the day the shelves fell on me.'

'That was. Funny.'

'So that was you laughing? It was terrifying.'

'The others ran. Away. That was even. Funnier.'

'And even more terrifying – I thought I was going to die, alone in the hangar.'

'I wouldn't. Have let. You.'

I asked her what had happened after that.

She said Eric had wandered around the hangar for a while, practising his walking.

'Then I went. Home. I was going to leave him here. Until I was. Ready.'

'Ready for what?'

'To Sell. Him.' Shatter had it all worked out in her head. 'Instead. Of people fighting each. Other and killing. People. We could have robot. Armies fighting robots. Could pay to watch. On TV. What do. You think? Eric could be. The first, and I'd be. Rich and Famous.'

'Eric's not a soldier. He likes making tea.'

'No. He's a. Soldier.'

'He wants to do the ironing.'

'He wants. Revenge.'

'*What?* What kind of revenge? What are you talking about?'

She didn't answer. A plane was passing overhead, so of course she was looking up at it.

'The Barcelona flight,' she said. 'I started to come here to watch. The planes go. By.'

The way she said it made it sound as if the planes were saying 'goodbye'.

'Why do you watch the planes?'

'One day I'll. Go home in. One.'

We were really close to the runway here. The Barcelona plane seemed almost to graze the tree tops, but instead of going in to land, it curved round, climbed higher and higher into the sky, then circled.

'It's supposed to. Land. Something's. Stopping it.'

'There must be some kind of problem at the airport.'

We looked at each other, and both at the same time said, 'Eric!'

We ran outside. I was going to head back along the path to the road, but Shatter grabbed me and spun me round before tearing off in another direction.

'Where are we going?' I shouted as I ran after her.

There was a bank of tall nettles right next to us. Shatter charged through it. She beckoned me to follow her. Stamping through nettles was fine for her with her resin foot. I wasn't so sure. Then I saw where she was heading. Something huge had flattened a path right through the middle of the nettle banks. the trail led through the trees ahead of us, all the way to the airport's perimeter. We could see a traffic jam of planes on the runway, a van speeding toward it with sirens blaring, and the Barcelona plane still circling overhead. We got a really good view of this because the part of the fence in front of us had been demolished. It looked like it had been ripped down like a piece of kitchen roll, screwed up and thrown aside.

We looked at each other. We didn't need to say 'Eric' this time. There was only one person who could have possibly have done that.

'Come on!' shouted Shatter.

Through the gap.

Across the grass.

We dashed for the buildings.

As we got nearer, we saw another van with a siren . . . and another. Alarms were wailing all over the airport runways.

'There's a. Situation!' Shatter said with a smile. 'There's going to be. Trouble.'

She said this the way you might say, 'There's going to be Viennetta.'

Then we saw him.

All the way around the perimeter of the main airport building, there are little bridges sticking out from the first floor, but ending in mid-air. Normally a plane taxis up to one of these, and the passengers board or disembark via the bridge. Eric was standing under the nearest one. As we watched, he pulled at the bridge's legs. They bent as easily as if they were made of marshmallow. He pulled the entrance to the bridge down until it was almost at ground level, then crawled inside.

'Where's he. Going?'

'He's looking for something,' I said. 'When he first went to the woods, he knew where he was going. He was going to find his leg.'

'SO . . .'

'Well, think about it. You're looking for something that you've lost in an airport. Where do you start?'

'I don't hang. Around in. Airports so. How would I. Know?'

'Lost Property.'

STEP 26: SEND HELP – QUICK

There was tension and fear all over the main concourse. Tension, because everyone could see that nearly all flights but one had been delayed. Fear, because everyone was worrying about why. I dodged and sidled through the crowd, with Shatter following me.

Every now and then, you'd hear the word 'robot' and 'rogue' or 'gone mad'. There were security people stopping anyone from going into departures or coming out of arrivals. Nobody even glanced at two kids going into the Lost Property reception.

It was quiet in there after the noise of the concourse. There was no one behind the desk but through the door at the back we could see a halo of light moving through the darkness of the shelves. Happy to Help was scrolling through something on her tablet.

'With you in one moment,' she sang.

I was going to answer her, but a different voice boomed out of the shadows.

I AM YOUR OBEDIENT SERVANT.

The voice of Eric!

'Are you really?' jeered Happy to Help. 'A servant is just what I need. Where have you been all my life?'

I'M SORRY. I CAN'T ANSWER THAT QUESTION.

'It's him,' I hissed to Shatter.

'I know. That.'

THERE ARE MANY LOST THINGS HERE.

'Tell me something I don't know,' murmured Happy to Help.

THERE ARE MORE LIFEFORMS LIVING ON A SINGLE HUMAN'S SKIN THAN THERE ARE PEOPLE ON PLANET EARTH.

'What?'

YOU REQUESTED THAT I TELL YOU SOMETHING YOU DIDN'T KNOW. I AM YOUR OBEDIENT SERVANT.

'Oh. Right. Trying to be funny. Very good.'

I WAS DESIGNED AND BUILT BY SHILLING OF SHILLING AVIATION.

'I'll be with you in one second. Why not take a seat?'

Oh, don't say that, I thought – but it was too late. There are seats in Lost Property, but they are fastened into the concrete floor with massive screws. But the woman had told Eric to take a seat, so Eric took one.

He stepped out of the shadows, blue eyes ablaze with electricity. Last time he'd been here, he couldn't stand up. Now he wasn't so far off reaching the ceiling.

Not going to lie, he did look quite frightening as he shook one of the chairs back and forth to loosen it, then wrenched it out of the ground with his massive hands. Chunks of concrete clumped to the floor. Metal fixings rang like warning bells.

Finally the woman looked up.

'*What? Who?* NO! Don't hit me!'

I dashed forward. 'He doesn't want to hit you. He's just doing what you said. He's a bit literal-minded, that's all. You said *take a seat*, so he took one. Please don't panic.'

But she was already lifting her CommsWatch to her mouth. She stared at me. 'You were in here the other day. Looking for a hand. Then you came back for a leg. Who are you?'

She didn't wait for a reply. She babbled into her CommsWatch, 'It's me. Lost Property. It's here. The Bad Robot. Come and get . . . Hello? Hello? HELLO? Oh, the reception in this place!'

I decided to plead with her. 'Please,' I said, 'don't worry. He's big, but he's gentle. He really is my obedient servant.'

Eric put the seat down and blinked.

I AM YOUR OBEDIENT SERVANT, he said.

The woman carried on frantically poking at her watch, trying to find a signal.

'Seriously,' I said, 'he just likes making tea.'

'He's a. Soldier,' Shatter said, beaming.

'He is NOT a soldier.'

'Why can't I get a signal?' howled the woman.

I carried on begging. 'Eric has made a few mistakes. But who hasn't? But before that . . . there's someone I'd like him to meet. It's my brother. He's in the high-dependency unit at Skyways St George's General Hospital.' I somehow thought that if I said the full name of the hospital, it would be more convincing.

'This thing attacked your brother?'

'No! No! Nobody attacked my brother. He was injured by a bus. So was I . . .' I held up Lefty to remind her of the first time we met.

'This thing tore your hand off?'

'No!' I was beginning to wish Tyler would show up to translate. 'My brother was in an accident. Now he's in a coma. I've been telling him all about Eric in his sleep. I think if he saw Eric, it might wake him up.'

'Ahhh,' said Happy to Help.

Was she starting to understand? Was she going to let us go?

I said, 'Please. For my brother. For Arthur.'

As soon as I said the name Arthur, Eric's eyes blazed blue and then dimmed.

'Ahhh, that's very moving,' said the woman. Then her phone beeped, and she cried, 'Lost Property. Send help quick! Armed help, if you've got it. Lots of armed help.'

While she was talking, Eric walked right past her desk, into the aisles of shelving. He was looking for something. We chased after him. But it was dark in there.

'It's dark. Very,' said Shatter, 'dark.'

We stood still, waiting for our eyes to get used to it. Little by little, we began to see the long avenues of shelves stretching away into the shadows. Slowly we walked along the first aisle, listening out for the grind of Eric's gears. Shatter kept stopping to squint at what was on the shelves.

'There's a. Coffin here.'

'I know.'

Some little thing began to glow near my elbow. Then it blasted out the music from Star Wars.

'A phone,' said Shatter. 'A box of. Phones. Someone just. Called a lost phone. Does this stuff ever. Get found?'

'I don't know. Shush. Hear that?'

Someone was rooting about in the shelves one aisle over. We dashed to the end of our aisle and doubled back on ourselves. And there was Eric, projecting beams of light through his own mouth and eyes as he stared into the shelves. He reached in and dragged something out.

'Eric,' I said. 'It's me, Alfie. Let's go . . .'

There was a sliding noise, then a ringing noise, then a swoosh of air. Eric had pulled something off the shelves. He'd found the thing he had come looking for.

A sword.

It was huge. It shone so brightly, we could read what was engraved on its blade: *Felix Culpa*. I did not have time to think about what the Shilling family motto was doing on it because Eric was already swooshing the sword as he hoisted it high above his head. It would have looked epic, except that the ceiling was NOT high above his head. In fact it was quite low. So, when he lifted the sword high, it went straight through the ceiling. Inside the ceiling were the electric wires that powered the lights and alarms for the Lost Property department. When the sword torched the wires, the lights and alarms went crazy, and the wires rained sparks and smoke into the room. Waves of blue light pulsed down the outside of his body.

Never had Eric looked so controversial.

STEP 27: ALFIE

Eric lowered the his sword to his side.

Even without the waves of electricity washing over him, he looked different. Something was changing in him.

'What's he. Doing? Is he going. To explode?'

'No,' I said, though I could see why Shatter was asking that. 'I think he's . . . remembering.'

He looked just like I felt on the day I remembered you, Arty. Like I was getting a memory upgrade.

'Finally,' said Shatter, 'he's got a. Weapon. Now we'll see some. Action.'

She was so right about that.

Eric turned and looked up at the hole he had made in the ceiling.

SORRY.

He turned his head towards me and said, **ALFIE**.

He'd never said my name before. It really was as if the sword had given him new powers. Maybe some of his memory or operating system was stored in the hilt.

He looked up at the ceiling again.

I CAN PERFORM SMALL HOUSEHOLD REPAIRS.

In one of the parallel aisles, I could hear the *tut tut* of Happy to Help's heels getting nearer. Looking up, I could see the little halo of light that followed her through her dark labyrinth. She was talking to someone. There were other footsteps alongside hers.

Reinforcements.

'She's coming,' I said. 'Let's get out of here.'

FARE THEE WELL, FAIR DAMSEL.

The footsteps stopped.

She'd heard us.

She was leading security right to us.

Eric gripped his sword. For a moment, I thought he was going to massacre them. Instead, he careered down the aisle in the opposite direction. We followed him past the coffin and the phones until he came to the 'Staff Only' door I'd used the first time I came to Lost Property. It was locked, but, to be honest, when you're talking about Eric, locks are not that relevant.

He pushed the door. It swung open.

We burst through it into baggage reclaim. After the dark of Lost Property, the light was blinding. I was expecting to run into a crowd of people, but there was no one there. Not a soul. The luggage carousels were all still. The information boards were blank. The great airport machine was switched off.

For a second, we just stood there in a kind of trance. Then Eric turned on his heels and strode towards the big doors that lead into arrivals.

'Eric! No!' I shouted.

Too late. They slid open as he approached them. On the other side was what looked like half the population of the planet, all staring expectantly.

They were not expecting Eric.

It was as though someone had pressed the mute button on the world. Then Eric swept his sword up from his side, into the air, in his outstretched arm. Somebody screamed. They all screamed. Not going to lie – some of them didn't scream. They took out their phones and filmed other people screaming.

Eric took a step forward. The crowd took a step backwards. The security guy with the big beard appeared.

'Who does this belong to?' he said, pointing to Eric.

I said, 'Eric doesn't belong to anyone.'

'What he's saying,' came a voice from the crowd, 'is just leave them alone and let them go.' It was Tyler. He'd come to the airport to see what the fuss was about. He came and stood with us.

'This unlicensed robot,' said Beardy Security, turning to the crowd, 'has delayed all your flights and created an atmosphere of panic. We wish to assure you that we are dealing the situation.'

A little figure literally leaped out of the crowd. It was D'Arcy.

'Let them go!' she yelled. 'Or else.' Then she did a few of her karate moves.

Here we all were, defending Eric.

FOR GLORY!

Eric strode towards the doors. The crowd jumped back. Eric could be pretty frightening when he was just waving a baguette around; with a real, actual sword, even I was terrified.

When Eric grabbed me by the collar and tucked me under his arm, someone in the crowd screamed, 'He's kidnapping that little boy!'

Someone else shouted, 'He's taking that kid hostage!'

I shouted back, 'He's just being cautious!'

No one seemed to hear – and, besides, when Eric left the building by walking straight through the plate-glass window, showering me with a million broken shards, I realized I was mistaken.

Outside, vans with sirens were powering up to the airport entrance. Eric held me up in the air for everyone to see. He really had taken me hostage. He was using me as a human shield.

Me! The kid who'd found his leg!

There was a shuttle bus waiting outside the airport. Eric dropped me on the pavement and clambered

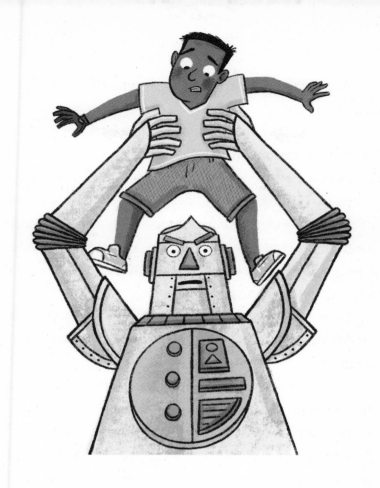

aboard. Before I could even stand up, the bus moved off. The sheer weight of Eric must have made the driverless bus think it was full. I watched it speed off, followed by a swarm of drones and, higher up, by a news organisation, thinking, *In four stops time, that will be outside Skyways St George's General Hospital. That's where Eric is headed.*

There was a woman standing alone on the pavement watching it too. I didn't even notice her until she turned to face me, eyes so wide you might think she'd just seen a flying elephant. Eyes so wide, in fact, that at first I didn't recognize her. It was Dr Shilling.

'That's impossible,' she gasped. 'It's HIM! That's the actual Eric.'

Before I could answer, people started pouring out of the airport on to the pavement, waving their phones around, wanting to film the robot. When they saw me, they crowded round, asking if I was all right. Did I need anything?

Someone noticed my hand and said, 'That is one cool hand, by the way. Can you move the fingers and stuff?'

Everyone agreed that it was a cool hand. I moved the fingers, and everyone applauded, and got their phones out again to film it or get a selfie with Lefty. I thought I was never going to get away. Then a hand reached through the scrum and yanked me out.

It was Dr Shilling.

'OK, Alfie Miles,' she said sternly, chivvying me towards the short-stay car park. 'Get in the car and tell me everything you know. We need to stop Eric before it's too late.'

STEP 28: ERIC VERSUS THE DRAGON

Dr Shilling drove frighteningly fast. Just after the airport, there was a police roadblock. She tapped the smart glass of her windscreen. It flashed the message 'Doctor on a Mission', and they waved us through.

All the way to the hospital, Dr Shilling ranted and raved. 'I don't believe it! You were sheltering that . . . machine. Do you have ANY idea how dangerous Eric is?'

'No.'

'But you must have heard the stories.'

'You said the stories weren't true. On the news. I heard you.'

'Of course I said they weren't true. Because they're not true. Not exactly. But Eric *is* dangerous.'

There was a helicopter hovering over the bypass.

'He's really polite, and he wants to be helpful,' I said.

'I'm going to tell you how dangerous he is. Before Grandad Shilling started making limbs for children, he built aeroplanes.'

'I know.'

'His wife – my grandmother, Honoria Shilling – was the test pilot. Their planes were so safe and so popular that the airfield grew into an airport. They were asked to showcase their latest plane – the *Shilling Excalibur* – at a special exhibition in London. Normally a king or a duke comes to open a big exhibition like that. But the engineers thought kings and dukes were things of the past. They were all about the future. So, two of them – Captain Richards and Mr Reffell – built a robot to perform the opening ceremony. A mechanical knight.'

'Just like Leonardo da Vinci?'

'Exactly. Richards and Reffell were Da Vinci in brown overalls. No one had ever seen anything like their robot. He could stand, sit, walk and talk. And when he talked sparks flew from his mouth because thirty-five thousand volts were shooting through his body. His name . . .'

'. . . was Eric.'

'Exactly. The Shillings were really thrilled with Eric. My dad, Arthur, was just a little boy then, and he queued for hours to shake the robot's massive hand. When he finally introduced himself, Eric looked him in the eye and said "Arthur? Like the king? Perhaps we could be friends?" My dad couldn't think of anything more amazing than having a robot friend.

'Eric was a sensation. Invitations poured in – New

York, Paris, Cairo, Valparaíso. In Buckingham Palace, Eric sang the national anthem for the king. Then suddenly – no one knew why – Eric disappeared. The world forgot about him. The history books say he was used as scrap during the war.' The doctor swerved around a slow car in front.

I almost said, 'Talking of history, we will be history ourselves any minute now if you don't drive a bit more slowly.'

But Dr Shilling did not pause to breathe. 'But Eric was not scrapped,' she said. 'The truth is Honoria Shilling found him. It was years later. My dad would have been about ten years old. Honoria was delivering a new plane to an airfield in the rainforest in Suriname. When she landed, the airfield was deserted. All except for a metal figure leaning against a tree. Birds had nested in his head. There was a sign stuck in the ground at his feet that read "Rust in Peace". Honoria recognized Eric right away. Eventually she found an old mechanic working in one of the hangars. He remembered Eric arriving years before and how excited everyone had been to see him. But the men who brought him – that must be Captain Richards and Mr Reffel – had been called away on urgent business. They'd promised to come back for Eric, but they never did. The mechanic seemed to think that that's what Honoria had come for. He helped her pack

247

Eric into her plane and she flew him back to Skyways.

'Of course, she tried to find Captain Richards, but he seemed to have vanished too. So, my dad, Arthur, and Eric finally could be friends. My dad and his father set to work. They gave Eric new batteries, oiled his joints, got him working. But they didn't stop there. They put light-sensitive cells in his eye sockets and taught him to see, using candles in beer bottles. They motorized his feet so he could shuffle. They kept on improving how he moved.

'All the ideas they got from working on Eric, they put into making new hands and feet for children who'd been injured in war or accidents. You could almost say Eric started the Limb Lab. Or, at least, inspired it.'

Dr Shilling smiled. 'Things got so busy, my grandparents programmed Eric to be a friend and guardian to their son – my dad. Eric could make tea and snacks . . .'

'I don't understand,' I said. 'Eric sounds really good. He looked after Arthur. He helped injured children. What are you worried about?'

'Eric was responsible,' said Dr Shilling, 'for the death of my grandmother.'

I gasped. '*What?* Eric – a murderer?'

Dr Shilling continued her story as we sped along the bypass.

'Eric got so smart, they began to wonder if they

could perhaps teach him to fly a plane. He'd be the perfect pilot of the future – a pilot who never gets tired, never makes mistakes. Or so they thought. They trained him to be a pilot. One day, Eric was flying a plane back from an air show with Honoria and my dad on board. As they got near to Skyways airport, Eric saw that the plane's approach was all wrong. The runway had been evacuated. So, Eric – pilot of the future – ejected from the plane. He shot into the air and crashed through the roof of one of the hangars. He left the plane without a pilot. It crashed. And my grandmother – she died that day.'

'Oh.' I didn't know what to say.

Dr Shilling drove even faster and took the bends even more wildly. 'She was a hero.'

'But . . .'

'There are no buts. She was a hero. And she died that day because of Eric.'

'But that wasn't Eric's fault . . .'

'A human pilot,' said Dr Shilling, 'might have flown off and tried again, but Eric calculated the risks and saved himself. As soon as he was in danger, he bailed out, leaving Honoria and Arthur to their fate.

'By some miracle, my dad, Arthur, was found wandering around the woods. After that, Eric was never mentioned again in the family. All photographs of him were destroyed. The hangar where he was built was closed up. Neither my grandad nor my father wanted anything to do with robots or aeroplanes ever again. They put everything they'd learned from Eric into the Limb Lab. They were able to forget about him.

'But now he's back. There's a pattern here, Alfie. Eric gets lost. Someone finds him. Fixes him up. Then he does something terrible. And I think he's about to do something terrible.'

STEP 29: A MESSAGE FOR ARTHUR

There was already panic in the hospital when we arrived. An announcement was telling people to leave quickly and quietly. It was hard to move against the flow of people exiting the building. Luckily Dr Shilling knew to use the emergency stairs to get up to the second floor.

When we clattered through the doorway, Eric was already up the corridor, marching towards HDU. His head was scraping along the ceiling, knocking the fluorescent light strips down one after the other. They swung from their wires like lightsabers wielded by invisible Jedi.

There were still lots of people in the corridor. Most of them were screaming and pointing as Eric stamped along. His sword's bright blade flashed as he walked, as though it was slicing and slashing the sunlight. He seemed not to notice the fuss and noise all around him. He seemed not to notice anything until he came to the play area.

The one with the big yellow dragon slide.

The dragon's big eyelashes and red-lipped smile did not charm Eric.

SUBMIT. His sword sang in his hand. **FOR GLORY!**

Eric swung the sword. The dragon's head bounced off the window and rolled a surprisingly long way back down the corridor.

... AND FOR ARTHUR!

He really said that.

While Eric was still fighting the dragon, I ran ahead. I tried to get to you before he did, to warn Mum and the doctors. I'd forgotten the door of the HDU was locked. I rang and rang on the bell. The door said, '*Please ring once only and wait for someone to answer. Remember our staff are busy. Thank you for your patience.*'

'I haven't got time to be patient!' I wailed.

By then, Eric was there. He didn't ring the bell once and be patient. He strolled through the door as if it were made of paper. We had to scrabble over the broken fragments to get in after him.

Above the storm of screams and shouts came:

I AM ERIC. YOUR OBEDIENT SERVANT.

Arty. Your brain activity flew up and down like a demented yo-yo.

WHAT IS YOUR NAME?

Someone said, 'Arthur.'

And for a moment, none of us understood that it was *you*, Arty. It was such a small sound.

It passed so quickly.

It meant so much.

Did it really happen?

'Did he . . .' said Mum, stepping closer to the bed. 'Did my boy . . . did he speak?'

Then I shouted, 'Eric! NO!'

Because Eric had grabbed the sword by its blade and swung its big blunted hilt towards you.

I shouted, 'Eric, stop!'

But Eric's limbs were making such a racket that I was drowned out. His knees squealed and cranked as he knelt down by your bed, the hilt of his sword pointing towards you.

ARTHUR. *FELIX CULPA!* he said, and he lowered his head.

Then the second amazing thing happened, Arty.

Your fingers closed round the hilt and held it tight.

There was no doubt this time. Your hand stayed on the hilt.

Mum gasped. 'Arthur – you moved your fingers. You moved! Good boy!' She put her hand over your hand and twined her fingers into yours, like a grown-up holding a toddler's hand when they're learning to walk.

The tiny doctor came in to see what was going on.

Mum looked up at her and grinned. 'He won't let go,' she said.

The tiny doctor was not even looking at Arthur. She was staring at Eric.

I HAVE ONE MESSAGE FOR ARTHUR.

How could Eric have a message for Arthur?

He spoke, but his voice was not his usual voice. It sounded like a woman trying to make herself heard over a burning engine . . .

IT'S THE FUEL LINE. IT'S BURST. THERE'S NOTHING WE CAN DO. SAVE ARTHUR. TELL HIM THAT I LOVE HIM, AND I'M SORRY. I'M PRESSING YOUR EJECTOR BUTTON NOW.

Just like the DustUrchin, Eric could save and repeat messages.

'Who was that?' asked Mum.

'My grandmother,' said Dr Shilling, her eyes glistening, looking as though she was about to cry. 'The Arthur she was talking about was my father.'

254

STEP 30: *FELIX CULPA...*

It took a while to work out
exactly what had happened.
I went back to the hangar
with Shatter and Tyler
and D'Arcy. We stood
next to the hole in
the ground and
looked up at the
legendary hole
in the roof.

'That's where Eric. Fell through,' said Shatter. 'And that's where he. Landed.'

'He fell through the roof and made a hole in the floor,' said Tyler.

'So it was Eric who made the legendary hole in the roof,' said D'Arcy. 'The roof broke their fall. So little Arthur got away safely.'

'Though he probably didn't know where he was,' I said. 'Or what had happened. Accidents can make big holes in your memory as well as in roofs.'

A plane flew over. Shatter said it was going to Dublin.

'Eric's knightly duty was to take care of Arthur. That was his noble quest.'

'His leg must have. Got stuck but that. Didn't stop him,' said Shatter. 'He left it behind and went. Looking for. The boy.'

'That explains why his leg was here,' said Tyler. 'But it doesn't explain how he ended up in Lost Property.'

'Of course it does!' I said. 'Eric takes things literally. He'd lost Arthur. Where's the most logical place to go looking if you've lost something?'

Tyler smiled. 'Lost Property.'

'While he was in there looking for Arthur, he slipped into battery-saving mode, and he stayed there. Everyone forgot about him. Like King Arthur asleep in his cave. They say King Arthur will wake up when he's needed. Well, I needed Eric, so he woke up. He was told to take a message to Arthur, and that's what he did. Just not exactly the right Arthur. I guess it's what you would call a happy accident.'

Mum keeps a notebook of all the times you open an eye or move a hand or say a word. The days that you do that get closer and closer together now. Sometimes, you do two or three on the same day. Sometimes I think you must feel like I do on a winter's morning, when it's time to get up, but I roll over and shut my eyes for five more minutes.

'It's exactly like that,' says Mum. 'Except it might take Arty five days, five weeks, five months. We don't know. And you know what? It doesn't matter.' She reached down and wound her fingers in with yours again. 'I could sit like this forever, as long as I know he's coming home.' She had a look on her face that I'd seen somewhere before. But I couldn't think where, just then.

STEP 31: I'M GOING. HOME.

Even after we found out that he didn't cause the crash, Eric was still controversial. There were consequences for sheltering and repairing an unlicensed robot. We were all taken to the Robot Decommissioning Authority for questioning. The Robot Decommissioning Authority was a very small man with very big teeth. When he smiled, it looked like his teeth were trying to run away and find a bigger mouth to live in. He asked us loads of questions. Then said the only absolutely safe solution was to take Eric to R-U-Recycling and put him in the crusher. 'This should have been done weeks ago,' he said. 'When Alfred Miles had the misfortune to discover this Eric thing in Lost Property.'

'No!' begged Dr Shilling. 'Eric was built with noble intentions. When the plane crashed, he was behaving nobly. Bravely. He saved my father's life. I wouldn't be here if it wasn't for Eric.'

'There are plenty of robots who can do anything that Eric can do far more quietly and efficiently and with far less squashing of police cars and disrupting of airports.'

'My grandfather built Eric,' said Dr Shilling, 'to protect my father. Thanks to Alfie, he has come down to me through the generations. He is like family. He's all the family I have. Please.'

The Authority agreed that Eric was a robot of historical interest and that Dr Shilling could keep him in the museum.

I was glad that he was not going to be destroyed but a museum? Really? Surely Eric was good for something more than being looked at.

A plane flew over.

'Twelve fifteen. From Sarajevo,' said Shatter. 'Wednesdays only.'

'How do you know that?' asked the Authority.

'Because next. Wednesday. I'm going to be. On that plane. Sarajevo is my home. I'm going. Home.'

'She's from Bosnia,' said Tyler. 'That's why her home is in Sarajevo, which is the capital of Bosnia. She had her foot blown off by a landmine during the war there.'

'Surely not,' said the Authority. 'The war in Bosnia ended in 1995.'

'But I stepped on. A landmine last. Year,' said Shatter. 'When my dad. And me were. Picking. Blackberries.'

'I always thought you were fighting in a war,' said D'Arcy.

'No. Picking. Blackberries.'

'The war was over before she was born,' said the Authority.

'You think. So?' Shatter glared at him. 'A war is only. Over when it stops. Hurting people.'

Which is when I had my great idea. I put my hand up. 'Eric's a knight,' I said. 'All he needs is a quest. I think I've got an idea.'

Dr Shilling took me and Mum to the airport to wave Eric off. Shatter was going with him. They had to turn off the metal detector so that he could go through Departures without setting off every alarm in the place. He introduced himself to all the security people:

MY NAME IS ERIC, THE WORLD'S MOST POLITE ROBOT. PERHAPS WE CAN BE FRIENDS.

Dr Shilling said, 'Goodbye and take care.'

Eric said, **I'M SORRY. I'M PRESSING YOUR**

EJECTOR BUTTON NOW.

Which made no sense unless you knew that he was speaking in the voice of Dr Shilling's grandmother. He was reminding her that he was sort of part of her family.

Then he looked at Shatter and said, **FOR GLORY!**

'See you some. Time,' Shatter said to me.

'See you sometime,' I replied.

And then they were gone.

We still need to keep talking to you to keep your brain patterns busy. We tell you what we're up to and what's happening in the world. Mum keeps a note of anything that makes your brain activity spike. The biggest spikes always come whenever we see Eric's quest on the news. Mum always brings a tablet in and plays the reports about ten times at maximum volume.

'At over six foot and weighing half a ton, Eric looks a bit different from the robots who clean our floors and deliver our pizzas,' said the news reporter. 'Some people have called him the Mechanical Knight, partly because he has courtly manners and partly because he looks like a gigantic suit of armour.'

The film showed Eric walking around a hillside somewhere, a group of people watching him from behind a Perspex screen.

'Look!' shouted Mum. 'Isn't that your little friend, the fierce one?'

Shatter was right at the front of the crowd. Dr Shilling was standing right behind her.

'This is one knight,' said the news reporter, 'who has found his quest!'

On the screen Eric took one more step and – *Blam!* – the ground beneath his feet exploded. Eric crashed to the ground.

'Yes!' said the news reporter. 'The mechanical knight has gone into battle against the scourge of landmines left over from the war. His method is very simple. He looks down at the location of the landmine and says, "**I AM ERIC. THE WORLD'S MOST POLITE ROBOT**", then he steps on the mine and it explodes.'

As she said the last bit, Eric staggered back on to his feet. His body was dented. His head had gone a bit wonky and his arm was hanging off.

'Poor Eric!' gasped Mum, holding her hands to her face.

'Don't worry about Eric,' said the reporter, as if he had heard her. 'With a bit of welding and some WD-40 the metal man can be made good as new. The man of steel is virtually indestructible.'

At the end of the report they interviewed Shatter. They said she'd invented Eric, but she put them right. She said her friend had found him and she'd helped fix him. We cheered when she said my name. And your brain activity peaked when we cheered. 'He's a. Warrior,' said Shatter, grinning with pride. 'He goes round fighting. For kids.' *BLAM!* 'So they. Don't get. Hurt I. Love explosions. Brilliant! We're going to. Travel all over. The world destroying land. Mines in Egypt, Cambodia, Uganda – you. Name it.'

After that they interviewed Dr Shilling. 'It was my grandfather,' she said, 'who originally repaired Eric. Many years ago. He would be so proud of the work that Eric is doing now to protect children all over the world. For many years Eric was missing. I'm so glad that Alfie Miles found him.'

The camera showed Eric inspecting his damaged arm. When he realised the camera was on him, he adjusted his joints and said:

A GENTLEMAN LOOKS HIS BEST AT ALL TIMES.

ARRIVALS

Sometime later. Maybe it was five weeks or five months.

Sometimes it seems a short time.

Sometimes it seems a lifetime.

Whichever, we went to the airport to welcome Eric and Shatter home. We waited in arrivals, clutching our 'WELCOME HOME, ERIC' sign.

Really waiting for someone feels very different from just pretending to wait for someone. You don't think about other people's food. You don't look too much at other people's faces. You just stay focused on those big doors, waiting for them to open.

Now I realised where I'd seen it before – that look that Mum had on her face when she sat on the end of your bed, watching over you. It's the look that people have when they're looking at those big automatic doors, waiting for someone they love to walk through them.

It's the look we had on our faces that afternoon at the airport.

We weren't the only ones with 'WELCOME HOME, ERIC' signs, by the way. Eric's famous now.

Everyone loves him for getting rid of landmines. But they love him even more for the explosive ways he does it. Eric's all over YouTube. You can get Eric mugs, gifs and ringtones.

When he finally came clunking through those big doors into arrivals, there was a thunder of applause and a lightning storm of camera flashes. I'm part human/ part machine. I'm a bit bionic. But Eric is part human too. His body is metal but it only works because we filled it with our imagination, and our memories, and our hopes. Also WD-40.

We waved our 'WELCOME HOME, ERIC' sign in the air. Not going to lie, it wasn't the biggest or the sparkliest sign there. I wasn't sure he'd even seen us. His huge blue eyes flickered over the crowd. Someone shoved me forward. People stood back to let me pass. Someone else shouted, 'Go on, Alfie!' Everyone seemed to know that I was the one who'd found Eric. Everyone thought I was the one he was looking for.

But I wasn't.

He looked past me.

He looked straight past Mum,

and D'Arcy

and Tyler.

Eric walked straight through the crowd, bent down and looked into the face of the person next to us.

WHO ARE YOU?

'I'm Arthur.'

Because it really was you. It was your first day out of the hospital.

HOW DO YOU DO?

'I'm doing OK,' you said.

I AM ERIC, THE WORLD'S MOST POLITE ROBOT.

'I know who you are.'

Eric held out his hand. You put your hand in his. He squeezed. You squeezed back.

The he held out his other hand. I put my hand in his. He squeezed. Lefty squeezed back.

'Let's go,' I said.

I AM YOUR OBEDIENT SERVANT.

Then we walked out of the airport – you and me and Eric.

AUTHOR'S NOTE

There really was a mighty robot called Eric, and he really was built by Captain W Richards and his friend Alan H Reffell. Eric made his first public appearance at an exhibition in London in 1928. Originally the Duke of York was due to open the exhibition, but when he couldn't make it Richards and Reffell decided to build a robot to take his place.

Eric's nervous system was four kilometres of wire. His skin was aluminium. His bloodstream was 35,000 volts of electricity, which made his teeth shoot sparks. He could stand, sit and answer fifty questions. He couldn't walk, though. Captain Richards liked to say this was because Eric was only six months old and hadn't learned to walk yet.

Mr Reffell imagined that Eric would be able to get a job – maybe answering the phone in an office, or giving out information in a railway station. But from his first appearance he was a sensation.

'Aluminium Man Startles London' ran one headline.

An American paper published a full-length interview with him, in which Eric revealed that he didn't drink, or smoke, or run around nightclubs at night.

'Girls!' declared the interviewer. 'Eric is the perfect man.' And he compared him to a chivalric knight.

Then, during the war, Eric disappeared. Maybe someone – worried he might be damaged during the bombing – hid him in a cellar for safekeeping. Eric was almost forgotten. Until, in 2017, the London Science Museum had an exhibition of all the greatest robots from history. The curator – Ben Russell – found some of the plans for Eric and asked the robot maker Giles Walker to rebuild him. He even let me come and see Eric while he was being rebuilt. It was an amazing experience. Thank you very much, Ben. And thanks to my son, Xavier, who came with me and asked much more interesting questions.

When Eric was first created, he looked like the future. By the time Ben and Giles rebuilt him, he was history. He was a mechanical Rip van Winkle. He fell asleep in a world where hardly anyone had seen a robot. When he woke up, the world was full of robots. But none of those robots looked anything like him.

As I type this, I can see a robot lawnmower wandering around next door's back garden nibbling the grass like a big plastic hedgehog. Modern robots come in all shapes and sizes – from next door's hedgehog to Oppy, the robot that roamed the surface of Mars taking photographs and rock samples for fourteen years. It only stopped when it was swamped in a Martian dust storm. Oppy's last message was, '*My battery is low, and it's getting dark.*'

We have robot checkouts in supermarkets, and robot cameras quietly watching our streets. The internet is run by a vast army of invisible 'soft' robots, who monitor our spending, translate languages, recommend books and holidays. More importantly, some of the things we have learned in making machines that act ever more like humans have in turn inspired us to make better and better artificial parts for our own bodies.

Prosthetic legs now often have Bluetooth to help regulate the speed and the length of your stride when you walk on them. They're also often made of carbon fibre, which feels warmer and more 'human' than wood or metal. Myoelectric and biometric technology uses signals from our own muscles to operate new hands and arms. Alfie's story was inspired by the true story of Daniel Melville's 'hero arm', which was built for him by Joel Gibbard and Samantha Payne's company Open Bionics, whose motto is 'welcome to the future, where disabilities are superpowers'. Daniel's amazing arm was based on the arm of his favourite hero: Adam Jensen, from the video game *Deus Ex*, and he was kind enough to talk to me about how it feels and what it takes to be part-bionic. Massive thanks to Daniel.

As well as speaking to a really bionic person, I also got help from a real robot-maker. His name is Professor Andrew Vardy and he teaches at Memorial University in Canada. His robots are the exact opposite of Eric – they're tiny, tame and very helpful to humans.

It's a pity, of course, that one reason we need to learn to replace human hands and legs is that humans spend a lot of time, money and technology injuring other humans. Shatila – like thousands of other children – lost her foot to an unexploded landmine. Landmines are planted during wartime, but they don't vanish or stop working when the war is over. They are a kind of terrible legacy – staying in the ground, hurting innocent people for many years afterwards. Shatila is from Bosnia – a place I visited shortly after the war there had finished in 1995. People were already trying to clear the landmines then. More than twenty years later that work is still not finished. There are landmines like this in countries as far apart as Cambodia and Somalia. Some of the landmines that are still dangerous in Egypt date back to the 1950s. They're still killing people today.

Of course, one of the good things that modern robots can do is help us get rid of landmines.

Eric wasn't really a robot. He was what we call an automaton. He couldn't go off on his own like Oppy. He couldn't make decisions like next door's lawn mower. But, by building him, Reffell and Richards made us think what a real robot might be like. This is always happening in science. Someone has to imagine what it would be like to fly to the moon before anyone starts building a rocket. Dreaming is every bit as important as building.

Modern robots do lots of good, important work. But they wouldn't exist if people like Richards and Reffell hadn't had fun playing about with ideas in an old garage in Surrey.

I knew nothing about Eric until my friend and editor Sarah Dudman showed me some clips of him speaking – you can still find them on YouTube. Normally Sarah reads my books when they're almost finished and shows me how to make them better. But this time she was there at the beginning as well as the end. When the idea got lost and started to rust – like Eric – she dug it out of its hiding place and sprayed it with WD-40, and got it going again. Thank you, Sarah – like never before.

Thank you too to the wise and patient Venetia Gosling, who let me keep going at this book until the story was right.

And of course to the mighty Steven Lenton, who brings all my imaginings to life.

About the Author

Frank Cottrell-Boyce is an award-winning author and screenwriter. *Millions*, his debut children's novel, won the CILIP Carnegie Medal. His books have been shortlisted for a multitude of prizes, including the Guardian Children's Fiction Prize, the Whitbread Children's Fiction Award (now the Costa Book Award), the Roald Dahl Funny Prize and the Blue Peter Book Award.

Frank is a judge for BBC Radio 2's 500 Words competition and, along with Danny Boyle, devised the Opening Ceremony for the London 2012 Olympics. He lives in Merseyside with his family.

About the Illustrator

Steven Lenton is based in Brighton and loves to illustrate books, filling them with charming, fun characters that really capture children's imaginations. As well as illustrating Frank Cottrell-Boyce's multi-award winning books, he is the illustrator of the bestselling and award-winning Shifty McGifty and Slippery Sam series. Steven also illustrates the Nothing To See Here Hotel series, the first of which won the Sainsbury's Children's Fiction Book Award 2018.

StevenLenton.com

DESTINATION:

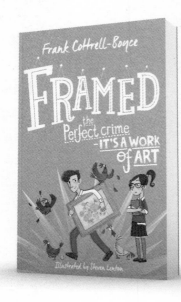

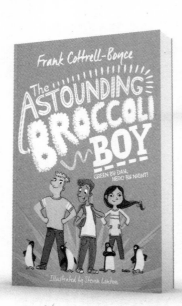

ADVENTURE!

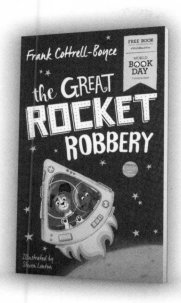

A world of possibilities